DRAGON BLESSED

AN IMMORTAL DRAGONS NOVEL

OPHELIA BELL

Dragon Blessed

Copyright © 2018 Ophelia Bell

Cover Art Designed by Jacqueline Sweet

Photograph Copyright © DepositPhotos.com and Period Images

ISBN-13: 978-1-955385-11-4

Published by Animus Press

UNITED STATES

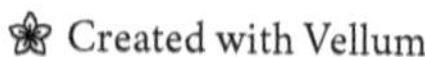 Created with Vellum

You've seen my descent. Now watch my rising.

— RUMI

CHAPTER 1

NEELA

Australian Outback, Four Days Prior to Spring Equinox

"We should have brought a dragon with us, I'm telling you."

Neela gave her brother a sidelong look as she rifled through the pockets of the unconscious Hunter at her feet, finding only lint. "You keep saying that. If I'd known you were going to be such a whiner about walking, I would have invited Sterlyn and Zamirah to come."

Naaz frowned. "It isn't the walking. I'm just fucking sick of getting ambushed by Ultiori every ten miles. We could've flown and been there weeks ago." He finished his own inspection of another Hunter and stood, scowling around at the latest unit of mind-controlled mercenaries they'd come across on what had become the mission from hell.

Neela toyed with the hilt of her blade. "This is the same unit that attacked us two days ago, and they're none the worse off for it. It'd take ten minutes to make sure they don't try again."

"They're victims like us, sis. And no match for us, either.

We get this mission done, we can free them from Meri's influence once and for all."

Neela let out a sigh and dropped her hand to her side, hoping that their mercy didn't come back to bite them on the ass. Again.

She turned her gaze back to the ocher landscape of the Australian Outback. At times a desolate wasteland, it possessed its own stark beauty. Today they'd hiked down into a canyon of iron-rich stone oxidized by the harsh climate into shades of red. She was surrounded by natural formations that reminded her of Red dragons in their sanguine majesty.

Reds weren't her favorite, though their closest friend was mated to one, and immortal Red blood ran through her brother's veins. The power that blood gave him was waning, as evidenced by the cut on his forearm he carefully tended now. One of the Hunters had landed a lucky blow.

Neela's own enhanced abilities wouldn't last, either. She'd been granted one last infusion of Belah's blood just before embarking on this quest, but that had been weeks ago, and while they'd managed to predict and fend off ambush after ambush on their way to the hidden dragon temple, it wouldn't last much longer.

Just two more days. That was all they needed.

"We have no choice but to walk, brother, and be on our guard for the next ambush, because I have a feeling this isn't the last we've seen of these guys. You may as well take a breath and enjoy the journey. Doesn't this landscape appeal to you?"

A trickle of sweat carved a path down her brother's temple, cutting through the layer of red dust to reveal the richer brown of his skin beneath. He was her mirror in so many ways, some identical and others her polar opposite. They could finish each other's thoughts, knew each other's deepest desires, and possessed the same unwavering determination to prove themselves. He was her best ally in a fight too, as their six unconscious enemies attested to.

Naaz turned his gaze to her, vivid blue eyes as much at odds with the dusty burnish of his skin as the bright, cloudless sky was at odds with the red landscape. "I wish I had your patience. When did you turn into such a wise woman?" The corners of his eyes crinkled, pieces of red flaking away with his smile to land on the dusty kerchief tied around his neck.

Neela couldn't help but smile back. "One of the necessities of being female, I suppose. It's a requirement to tolerate the men in my life."

Naaz's laugh was deep and rich. "Are we that much of a trial? Perhaps *he* will be different."

A knot twisted in Neela's gut and she shifted her gaze back to the path before them. Zorion was still an enigma, despite his occasional mental visitations that had begun not long after she'd first learned of his existence. She quickened her strides, impatient to end their journey and meet her dragon in the flesh.

"Zorion *is* different, but maybe not the way you're suggesting. He's nothing like you, and I doubt his sister is anything like me."

Naaz raised a brow as though he were about to make some quip. Then he pressed his lips together, thinking better of speaking the words. He was always better at holding his tongue than she was.

"They are ours, regardless," Naaz said. "I doubt they are like anything that exists in the world ..." His throat rippled with his effort to swallow. "Asha is ..." He trailed off and shook his head.

"She's your mate."

He nodded and gave Neela a small smile that betrayed his

helplessness. She had the same feeling of desperation clawing at her, the same driving need to get there as soon as possible. Only part of it was due to the conflict raging between their allies and their enemies. The repeated attacks she and Naaz had endured during their journey didn't help. The dragons she and her brother were seeking could turn the tide of this war, but that prospect did nothing to diminish her and her brother's need to finally be with their mates.

They'd been forced to wait nearly three thousand years for this. Barring any more ambushes, they were only two days out from the temple where their dragons lay in hibernation. But two more days felt like two days too many. Marveling at the scenery was the only way Neela managed to pace herself on this trek through an unforgiving landscape.

The dreams didn't help ease her agitation. Zorion had been in her head ever since she and Naaz had come across their ancient temple long ago during a quest for their master. She'd been drawn to the chamber on some remote, desolate island in the middle of the ocean, and she and Naaz had drifted there, answering a call they'd both heard. But they'd barely had the chance to set eyes on the pair of statues—barely dared to touch them—before Nikhil had tightened the vise of his control on their minds and forced them to stand down.

That had been the beginning of the end of their loyalty to their *Sayid*, and their subsequent rebellion ultimately forced their master to imprison Neela just to keep Naaz under control. It had taken centuries before they understood that the man they saw as a second father to them was being influenced by something much stronger and more insidious than they could ever understand. It was only within the last year that they'd discovered the true identity of the creature who had kept them imprisoned and conducted vile experiments on them.

She and her brother were still complicit in Nikhil's vicious acts, though. They'd been his tools at the beginning, killing out of loyalty to him long before their minds were affected by the monster who controlled him. Dragons had died at their hands, though far more were imprisoned and tortured after Neela and Naaz had become slaves themselves, rather than soldiers.

There was a fine line between the two, she realized. That line was choice, and the moment Nikhil had hidden their mates away from them was the moment their choice had been removed.

Now that their beloved *Sayid* had his mind back, he had released them. And having their freedom restored, they had both chosen to remain at his side, despite that ever-present need to find their mates. Neela had managed to hone her self-control during her thousands of years of imprisonment. The urge to bloody her fists on the doors of an impervious prison never went away, but she learned not to act on those urges after discovering it did no good. Their true jailer was far too powerful a creature to fight alone.

CHAPTER 2

NEELA

Neela's dreams of Zorion were nebulous things. At first she thought they were only reflections of her own frustrations of being locked away, until after the first time she'd been taken to a lab and used as one of the Ultiori's breeding specimens. It was only a simple medical procedure, the technician clinical and detached while completing her task. She hadn't known at the time, but the woman performing the procedure had been the vessel of the enemy—the creature that had hold of Nikhil's mind—and her goal was to use Neela to create a hybrid offspring for her own contemptible purposes.

Something changed that night, and ever since, the dreams that came were of a creature who knew nothing of itself, yet knew Neela had been used for some inhuman purpose. He spoke to the part of her mind that had been broken by the invasion, showed her a reflection of her own self-hatred, took it into himself, and made her whole again.

And every time after that, when she was forced to take the seed of a stranger against her will, her visitor would wrap her in the comfort of his velvet oblivion and make the pain and despair go away. Each time, he vowed to avenge the wrongs done to her when he was released from his prison.

That night, when she and her brother made camp, she lay gazing into the fire, acutely aware of the pull of Zorion's magic. That same velvet oblivion beckoned from somewhere in the night, deep inside the temple where Zorion and his sister had been relocated only a few months ago. But this time when she reached him, she'd actually get to see him, to touch him in the flesh.

"I feel you near me, adara," he rumbled into her mind as she drifted off. *"The stars tell me you are but another day away."*

"Will you show yourself to me in dreams tonight?" Neela asked, hoping for a hint of his desire. His use of the pet name he'd given her ages ago warmed her, but she was disappointed by his evasive answer.

"You see my soul more clearly than any but my sister. I am ready for you to find me."

"We're traveling as quickly as we can."

A hush crept over their connection, and Neela's gut tightened.

"The temple is perilous and dark. Be careful when you enter," he replied before receding from her consciousness.

His absence left her confused, wondering what she might have said to make him withdraw. Normally he would have lingered through the night as though standing watch over her slumber. Not once had he made more overt advances, though she'd always sensed a deep curiosity.

In her dreams, he barely ever touched her, only venturing as far as a brush of a shadowy fingertip down her cheek. The dreams themselves were as dark as an abyss, the only thing differentiating them from deeper sleep being the awareness she had of his presence within that void. Sometimes she could almost make out a shape, big and dark. She'd begun to fill in the blanks in her mind, and he became an ebony guardian, his black skin shot through with veins of opalescent color, his eyes prismatic fire.

Despite the lack of contact, her body burned hot whenever he was present within her consciousness. She longed for his touch disconnected from the violent acts he'd always guarded her mind from. He may have never made love to her, but he'd been even closer than a lover countless times during all those vile experiments she'd been subjected to.

For decades, Neela had endured the invasion of the clinical procedures—the impersonal injections of some anonymous donor's seed into her womb on the days when Meri believed she was fertile. None of those sessions bore fruit.

Then one day she found herself hauled into the lab and strapped down to the table, feet stuck in cold stirrups and knees spread. But the doctor didn't sit between her legs with the usual instruments. Instead, a pair of burly Hunters hauled a struggling, naked male through the door, his face screwed up in rage and fear. She didn't recognize him, but knew from the sparking storm in his eyes that he must have been a turul captive.

"This won't work!" she yelled, cold rage seeping into her bones when she realized what they intended. Before she could protest further, a gag was shoved in her mouth and fastened at the back of her head.

"Cover her face," the doctor commanded, and panic set in when they shoved a cloth sack over her head.

She groaned and struggled against her bindings, forcing a muffled scream through her gag when the cold lubricant was squirted on her nethers. Hot tears streamed down her cheeks when the other captive entered her, his movements jerky and without rhythm until he let out an agonized grunt and his cock fully hardened. Whispered apologies fluttered around her ears like tiny moths, repeated over and over in the air between his hot breaths gusting over her throat.

Nausea threatened to purge her belly of its contents, her entire being rejecting the experience. Then in the midst of her despair, Zorion's comfort enveloped her, driving away all sensation of the room she was in and the horror of the forced breeding she endured. His whispers eased her, calmed her, and she drifted away into the escape he offered.

"I would become him if I could," he had said. *"Make love to you the way you deserve."*

"No. I never want to associate these moments with what I wish you were to me. When I'm with you, it will be different."

"When we are together, you may not wish so hard for my touch. You do not know me in the flesh, Neela. I am not like you—not small and beautiful. I am a monster."

"Anything you do would be better than this."

He'd maintained his distance from the physical ordeal of those experiences, but kept his promise to block them from her mind. He became her soul's protector from the things she had to endure, and kept her sane for the endless days of her imprisonment.

It had been the touch of another who she loved that finally lit the spark of longing in her to feel Zorion's touch. Barely five months had passed since Meri had sent Nikhil to her. Neela wondered if it was because she trusted Nikhil and knew Neela did too.

Neela had immediately seen the struggle in her *Sayid's* dark eyes when he first entered her cell in the Alexandria Institute's Canadian facility. While she couldn't hear what went on inside his head, his gritted teeth and clenching fists made it clear he was at war with the creature who controlled his mind.

Finally, he had let out a long sigh and opened his eyes. They were clear of the inky influence of their captor, and he gave her a tortured look. "We have no choice, goddaughter. I will be gentle, but if you need to escape as you do in the lab, I understand."

Looking at him that day, she knew she couldn't hide from the experience. "Do you know you are as much a prisoner as I am?" she'd asked.

Nikhil raised a finger to his lips and shook his head. "There are secrets that the blue sky cannot see, but the darkness reaches everywhere eventually, and sometimes overstays its welcome. Let us both have this moment of light while the darkness is distracted."

When Zorion's presence hovered at the back of her mind, ready to shield her from another horrific encounter, she silently communicated her willingness to remain present—the Nikhil in the room with her was the one she remembered from childhood, not the sadistic puppet who did their master's bidding.

Nikhil waited for her answer with a patient, silent plea, unwilling say more, lest the darkness hear him. If he were willing to be here in this moment with her to carry out this act neither of them wished for, she would at least share the ordeal with him. He may not have been the man she wanted to be with, but he was someone she loved, and that counted for something.

She couldn't interpret the shadowy fluctuations of Zorion's presence once he understood her decision, but he stayed where he was, a silent observer while Nikhil made love to her.

Afterward, she'd lain alone in the pitch dark of her cell, and Zorion spoke to her once more. *"Someday I will be the one to touch you as he did, to give you those feelings you felt for him. Someday I will be the one you love,* adara.*"*

Neela had taken a deep breath, rolling over and reaching into the darkness, imagining she could brush her palm over his dark cheek. *"His touch pales in comparison to how you make me feel with just a thought."*

His shadow warmed and grew heavy beside her, her palm tingling with the contact of what felt like smooth skin instead of empty air. Vivid colors sparked like tiny bolts of lightning, arcing over his face to give hints of the contours and lines of a straight nose, strong jaw, and full lips.

Neela's heartbeat quickened. This was more than just a thought, this warm, almost solid presence in her small bed beside her. She still couldn't quite make out his features—they disappeared into the darkness when the little veins of light faded between pulses that matched his pulse.

The darkness shifted, grew denser near her face, and she closed her eyes and sighed as his warm fingertips traced a line over the edge of her jaw. His breath gusted over her lips, mouth a hair's breadth from hers.

"Is this real?" she asked the presence inside her mind. Her entire body ached for him to close the distance. She didn't dare move lest she shatter what she was sure must be a hallucination.

"Am I here with you? No, it is only an illusion. If I could escape my prison fully, I would not leave you trapped in yours. What I can do is make you feel anything you desire with only a thought," he said. *"What is your wish, adara?"*

"Kiss me," she breathed.

He'd pressed his palm more heavily against her cheek, slid it around to the back of her neck, and pulled her to him until her mouth met his. Neela hadn't cared that he wasn't really there. His presence was believable enough for her to let herself forget.

When the velvet heat of his tongue pushed into her mouth, she moaned and leaned close, slipping her hand from his cheek, down his shoulder, and back up, reveling in his form. She explored his shape as they kissed, keeping her eyes closed, lest the illusion shatter under too much scrutiny.

Zorion's touch was more than she could have hoped for, and he explored her with as much languid fascination. He brushed his hand down her arm and dropped it to her hip, then glided it back up, leaving a trail of bright desire as he went. Neela hadn't dressed after Nikhil's departure and still lay naked on her small bed. Clothing mattered little in the dark isolation of her cell.

She let her hand slide up his neck and encountered no resistance. His scalp was entirely bare and smooth. And when she moved her hand lower, exploring the hard muscles of his chest, she found he was completely bare there as well.

He slipped his hand between them, brushing his fingers over the bare tip of her breast and sending a zing of pleasure to her core that made her gasp. He jerked his hand away with a soft grunt of surprise.

"I am sorry," he said, his voice still only echoing inside her mind.

"Don't be. It felt good."

"Indeed. You feel different than I imagined."

His statement gave her pause. "You ... can feel me? I thought you were just a figment of my imagination."

Warmth returned to her breast, his big palm cupping again, even more gently this time.

"Just because my body isn't physically with you doesn't mean my mind is absent. It's like a waking dream we both share."

"That's ... nice ..." She let out a soft sigh, losing track of her thoughts as he gently closed his hand over her breast and his fingertips drew together, slipping along her skin until only her nipple was held between them. He swirled his fingers in a circle around the hard tip until she squirmed.

He bent again and captured her mouth with his, kissing her slowly. Then he grew bolder and moved down her body, mouth tracing a hot line along her sternum until his tongue reached her breast and teased her nipple. She opened her eyes to the disorienting sight of opalescent fire sparking in the shape of a tongue.

"*Is it unusual that I wish to taste you?*" he murmured, sucking her nipple into his mouth.

"No. I like that."

"*I can feel your pleasure. It makes me ache in ways I don't quite understand. Like a hunger and a need to provide food at the same time. I want to both devour you and give you sustenance.*"

He moved his mouth lower, the heavy shape of his body hovering over her while his lips tickled a tantalizing path down her belly, his big hands rubbing up and down her sides. Neela's core throbbed and heated in anticipation of him reaching her there, but then she remembered where she was and what she'd been doing mere moments before he'd returned.

"Stop!" she yelled, sitting up and abruptly pushing him away.

A painfully beautiful image of a man flashed before her eyes before the fire died and he faded back into the shadows. But she'd seen the hurt in his eyes before he went. Her heart ached at the way he withdrew from her.

"*I am sorry,*" he whispered.

"Please don't apologize … I'm the one who's sorry. It isn't your fault, I just can't be with you like that yet. I want to, but … you don't want me right after I've been used the way I have. I'm not clean."

"*I will always want you, adara. You are mine. The baby he put inside you tonight is half you, which makes her half mine to love and protect. The feeling you have right now makes no sense. You are not tainted because you let yourself be loved under duress. It shouldn't stop you from loving freely when you wish.*"

She blinked at the pulsing network of veins she made out

in the dark. It didn't make her feel any better that he still wanted her, regardless of the fact that she was still marked by another man's essence. Nikhil's seed still coated her thighs. She closed her eyes as the rest of Zorion's little speech sank in.

"Please, no ..." she said, sinking back down to the bed. She pulled the pillow to her chest and buried her face in it, struggling to hold back tears. "Tell me you were guessing ... that the baby doesn't really exist."

It is only a spark, but there is life in your womb. Why does this make you sad?

"Because it means Meri will have what she wants."

"The creature that took my mother's love from her," he stated flatly. *"The one who is keeping us apart."*

"Yes. And there's nothing we can do about it."

His comforting warmth enveloped her again, as though he embraced her from behind. He said no more, only held her while she cried, grieving the eventual loss of a child she'd never even imagined might exist, or that she'd even care about so much.

After that night, Zorion had refrained from intimate contact beyond holding her as she cried. When Meri eventually did magically spirit the tiny fetus from her womb, he was there, but not even his presence was enough to comfort her through that loss. He couldn't tell her where it had gone, or even if it survived. His link was with her, and her alone.

The closer they got to the temple, the more that night came back to her. How very solid and warm he had felt, more tangible than the many faceless males who had been forced to breed with her to no effect, or even Nikhil himself, whose deliberate tenderness had been so clearly at odds with his true desires. She knew her *Sayid* was a brutal sadist at heart, and the one time they coupled he had behaved against his true nature for her sake.

She didn't regret stopping Zorion from pursuing more intimate contact with her that night, but the closer she got to him, the more she craved knowing what it would have felt like to have his mouth on her everywhere, to have him spread her legs wide and bury himself inside her, to have him push her limits the way she wished Nikhil had done.

Her dreaming mind fixated on those remembered sensations of Zorion's deft hands instinctively understanding what would give her pleasure, and of how much his body responded whenever she arched into him or vocalized her ecstasy. She couldn't actually see his body, but she had felt the strength of him from head to toe, and particularly the thick, rigid heat of the cock that had brushed down her body as he'd slid lower on his quest to please her.

But when awake, she doggedly marched onward, her focus on following the tether of power that joined them. When she reached him, there would be no limits, no boundaries, even if his very touch burned her alive.

CHAPTER 3

NEELA

The morning of their last day of trekking through the terra cotta wasteland, Neela and Naaz packed up camp in silence and got moving without so much as a word. They rarely needed words to understand each other, and it wasn't until he touched her gently on the shoulder later that day when they stopped for water that she realized they hadn't yet spoken all morning.

She glanced up to see her brother's dark brows creased.

"We're not losing each other," she said, replying to the unmistakable worry she sensed in him.

"You're already gone, sis," he said. "But it isn't just you … My own mind has been in another place all morning."

"She's in your blood, isn't she? That want you can't shake, like a hunger that grips you so strongly your teeth hurt, and you know the ache won't leave until you get to have a taste …"

Naaz's dark lashes fluttered closed and he licked his lips, his cheeks darkening to a ruddy shade. "Don't …"

Neela gave him a perplexed look. "Brother, are you actually embarrassed? What happened to the cocky boy who used to brag about his skills to make women beg for more?"

His eyes flashed with irritation. She'd seen him in action countless times before they'd first encountered their dragon mates. Women responded to him easily and eagerly, and he'd never gone long between lovers. That had been a long time ago, though, and they both knew it.

"Evie was the only female I haven't had to use my powers on in centuries," he said softly. He squatted down at the edge of the spring and dipped his canteen into it. "It feels strange going to a female who actually wants me ... not my best friend's lover who has no choice, or any number of female captives who would probably rather die than have me fuck them."

The venom in his tone betrayed a level of self-loathing Neela had believed she was alone in feeling. She squatted back down beside him and stroked a hand over the bunched muscles of his broad shoulders.

"You made sure they enjoyed it."

Naaz grimaced. "The fact that I compelled their minds to *like* it doesn't excuse what I was forced to do. The closer I get to Asha, the more I feel like I should just turn around. Walk off into the desert and let her have a man who's worth something."

Neela's chest tightened at his utterly defeated tone. She remembered the horrified look in that first turul's eyes when the attendants had shackled his wrists above his head and manually stimulated him until he was hard enough to enter her.

"Fuck or die, you piece of shit," one of them had said. The last thing she'd seen before her face was covered by the hood were the tears in his storm-filled eyes.

Her brother hadn't been bound; that much he'd shared

with her. But he'd been compelled, nonetheless. He'd chosen to obey for her sake, and ultimately, she for his.

"I love you, Naaz," she said softly, leaning her cheek against his strong shoulder. "What was done to us was inexcusable, but *we* are not to blame. Do you blame Nikhil for everything, now that he's on our side?"

He picked at a stray thread on the pocket of his cargo shorts where a button was once attached. "Not anymore. If Belah could forgive him … if Iszak and Lukas could … and hell, Evie and Marcus … then I can too."

"Evie forgave you."

"That was different."

"Was it? Just because the three of you psyched yourselves into liking it doesn't make it right that you had to do it. None of us had a choice, brother. That's what you need to get through your head. If we didn't go willingly, Meri would have gotten into our minds and made us go through with it anyway, and she wouldn't have cared if it hurt."

He shook his head, close-cropped black hair shining with sweat in the late afternoon sun. "No. It was me too. I performed like a fucking champ for them. There were moments when Meri would urge me on, and I got this *rush* just knowing I'd pleased her, like I'd been a good pet. I wanted more of that feeling. What the hell does that make me, besides a filthy fucking piece of shit for ever, *ever* feeling good about what I was doing?"

"That's what Meri does," Neela said. "It's how she keeps her Hunters in line."

"But you know her blood meld never really worked on us. None of the Elites were affected beyond letting her hitch a ride once in a while. That's why she had to lock you up—or Evie, or Zamirah—to keep me and Marcus and Sterlyn in line."

"I don't care if she couldn't influence you with her magic.

She could still get into your head. She'd never have kept Nikhil under control for so long if she didn't have other tricks." Nikhil had been different, but Neela was never quite sure how. Meri had control of him long before she was aware of the woman's influence over any of them.

Naaz remained silent for some time, watching a droplet of condensation travel down the surface of his canteen. The shadows were lengthening now, portending sunset, and they were close enough to the temple that Neela knew neither of them would want to stop to camp for the night.

"I wonder if he knew all along but just didn't care. He changed after the blood exchange ... Did you notice that?"

She lifted her eyebrows. "Um ... that was a long time ago, but yeah, I remember. Hard to forget seeing you infused with all that Red dragon power. That was when the killing stopped and the breeding experiments started. And every time I saw him in the lab after that, it was like he'd been lobotomized."

"He found out Belah was alive. Knowing that changed everything. That's when I knew it wasn't him controlling us all along. That it had to be Meri. She was the only other person left from before. Even when she switched bodies, you always knew it was her from her eyes. I wonder what Nikhil would have done if he'd been in control."

Neela's gaze drifted to the distant edge of the pool. An underground spring had forced its way through the cracks in the granite and gradually worn out a deep depression in the stone over eons. It was rare for her to come across pieces of the world that she knew without a doubt were older than her and her brother. Places like this comforted her because they reminded her of the way they'd been shaped by time and circumstance, worn away by their experiences until nothing remained but their raw, primal essence.

"He'd have found her. And he did find her. And she forgave him. Have you talked to Asha about this at all?"

Naaz tensed and shook his head. "We don't have the same link you have with Zorion. And even if we did, she's too good to hear the details. How the hell would I start that conversation, anyway? 'Hey, baby, are you cool with my filthy, rapey prick being the one to wake you up?' She's too fucking good for me."

"Nikhil wouldn't have told us where she was, if he believed that. You trust him, don't you?"

He turned and looked directly into her eyes, his lips pressed into a line. "Do you?" he asked, and in his gaze she saw a challenge that made her heart plummet into her gut. He knew.

"He didn't force me, if that's what you're thinking. *She* forced *him* to come into my cell that night. Same as you and Sterlyn and Evie. Or Marcus … You know what, forget it. I'm not having this conversation with you."

She plunged her canteen back into the water to refill it one more time, then stood and stalked away. Hot tears pricked at her eyes. They'd all been coerced into couplings they'd never have entertained, had they been free to choose, but the saving grace of those few were that she actually cared about the men who came to her, even if she didn't love them.

The world in front of Neela blurred as she made her way down the path. She swiped angrily at the tears on her cheeks until the warmth of a familiar presence floated over her mind.

"We'll find her," Zorion said.

Neela nodded, sending back her silent gratitude.

"I'm sorry," Naaz said, falling into step beside her. "I guess I just feel like this is too easy."

Neela snorted. "Being forced into slavery and having to wait three thousand fucking years to be with the people we love? You're a good person, you idiot. What Meri forced you to do hasn't changed that. You. Had. No. Choice."

Naaz frowned and shot a sidelong glance at her.

"Well, sure," she said, answering his unspoken commentary. "You could've let them torture me, but you didn't. I forgive you, you shithead. Now would you just forgive yourself so you can finally be happy?"

He shook his head. "Not enough, sis. I can't help it."

She threw up her hands. "Fine. But I'll be damned if I let you ruin this for me. Tell Asha if she needs to commiserate over what a knucklehead you are, I'm here."

"Thanks, I think," he said, quirking his mouth at her.

Neela chuckled. She bumped him with her shoulder and he slipped his arm around her, holding her against him as they trudged along, their steps perfectly in sync as always.

"I love you," he whispered against the top of her head.

"Me too," she said, and let out a long sigh.

"Maybe I spoke too soon," Naaz muttered under his breath.

His skin prickled with a sense of unease. The red rock canyon they trekked through suddenly felt too exposed and he glanced up, surveying the rim several hundred yards above them. He saw nothing out of the ordinary. Just more scrubby weeds and dust silhouetted against the night sky.

"More fucking Hunters?" Neela murmured.

"Meri sure isn't fucking around about recapturing us. Do you have enough juice for another fight?"

"I'll manage. It takes skill as much as magic to kick their asses, and we've got centuries of practice on most of them."

Naaz's power was fading, but he had enough for another fight or two yet. He unsnapped the closure on the scabbard at his hip and closed his fist around the hilt of his knife. His gaze tracked a multitude of movements at the edges of the canyon, senses almost as acute as a dragon's picking up the signature of human auras.

Auras with the unmistakable taint of Ultiori Hunters. These ambushes were becoming almost predictable.

As with the last ambush, and all the others before that he'd lost count of, the Hunters were far from stealthy when they launched over the edge of the canyon. Five men bellowed the same ridiculous roars as they attacked. Two of them rushed Naaz, and he deflected the blow of a machete from one almost by rote, knocking the man back with a kick before spinning to avoid a knife attack from another. The other three fought bare-handed with his sister, who slashed out at them with her blade, ducking and spinning as though this fight was a well-rehearsed dance.

He wondered yet again at the lack of weapons of the three Neela fought, but something had bothered him about the behavior of her attackers. It was as though they sought to subdue a wild animal, to tame rather than hurt, while he felt like the Hunters he fought actually aimed to kill.

"I'm not fucking holding back this time!" Neela yelled, and for the first time, Naaz was willing to agree with her. He may not have felt worthy of presenting himself to Asha yet, but he'd be damned if his sister was forced to endure these setbacks any longer.

Hunters weren't always predictable fighters, but Naaz and Neela had originated many of the tactics themselves when they were members of Nikhil's Elite. Within moments, Naaz's attackers lay bleeding to death in the dirt, and he quickly helped Neela dispatch the other three.

Afterward, they sat catching their breath on a nearby rock, staring at the bodies. "This makes no sense," Neela said. "They didn't try that hard to survive. Hunters are usually more ruthless and less reckless than that."

"If they're after the temple, they'd need us to get inside. No sense killing their only way in."

"Meri has to know she's better off leaving Zorion and Asha in stasis. It would make more sense to try to kill us, and those guys definitely weren't aiming to kill."

"Speak for yourself," Naaz said, dabbing a dusty rag at a rend in his shirt where the one Hunter's machete had sliced through to his ribcage just beneath his heart.

Neela stared silently at his bloody shirt, her skin growing ashen. She swallowed and looked away, her mind throwing off adamant denial that Naaz couldn't help but pick up. She was afraid of being taken and forced to breed again.

"I won't let her have you," he said with steel in his voice. "And when you've awakened Zorion, he'll protect you too."

She turned her gaze to him once more. "How can I be the only female capable of doing what she wants? Why did it have to be *my* baby she took?" She shook her head, her jaw tightening. "Fuck, that sounds so selfish. She did take others. I know. But mine was the one that survived. Can't that be enough?"

"They didn't ever tell me how many times my seed took. But Marcus and Sterlyn and I were the most popular studs. Something about Elites makes us the best breeders for what she needs, perhaps."

"Oh, god. Do you think that means she recaptured Nikhil or one of the others? I'm the only female. If she already has a male ..."

"If that's happened, all the more reason for us to get moving to the temple."

Naaz sheathed his knife and stood. His sister pressed her lips together and slipped off the rock, falling into step beside him once more.

The buzz of energy in his mind flared brightly when he refocused on it, like a light at the end of a long tunnel. His awareness of Asha's presence in the world had been a beacon for months, ever since Nikhil had finally retrieved the pair from the hidden temporal pocket where he'd kept them. She was so close now he could sense her clearly in his mind. But with each step closer, his uncertainty grew.

Asha was a treasure far greater in value than a man like him deserved. She would be better off if another man awakened her. But he pressed on, because seeing his sister happy meant more to him than hiding his own shame.

They would all know at the end how unworthy he was, but at least Neela would be safe and happy in the arms of her dragon.

"Where the hell are you going?" Neela asked. "The temple's this way."

He stared down the path leading deeper into the canyon, the bright star of Asha's power beckoning to him like a flame. "No … it's this way," he said.

Neela propped her hands on her hips and shook her head. "The fuck it is. It's this way." She tilted her chin up a steep, rocky incline that led out to the starlit wasteland above.

"There's only one temple, sister. It's this way. I'd bet my life on it."

"Then you'd be dead, because there's no fucking doubt in my mind Zorion is that way." She jabbed a finger up to the edge of the canyon.

The shadow formed so swiftly at his sister's back, Naaz didn't have time to yell a warning before she went down. Then they surrounded him, the scent of blood and dust filling his nostrils.

If he didn't know better, he'd think his attackers were the same men he and Neela had left as corpses a few miles back. This time, the attack happened too fast for him to ward off, his movements growing slower and clumsier the more he fought.

When one of the Hunters knocked his legs from under him, he struggled to rise. His body felt leaden, as though gravity was his enemy. He yelled out a frustrated curse and turned his head, frantic to see what had become of his sister.

A huge, dark shape loomed over him, nearly indistinguishable from the night sky, save for the way it blocked out the stars. What Naaz could see was not quite a man, though it had the outline of one. It was pure, shining black, save for iridescent veins flickering over the surface of the exposed skin above its waist.

The creature crouched beside Naaz and tilted its head, its obsidian eyes flaring with strange multi-hued fire.

"You have a choice." The sound was in the air, reverberating around Naaz's entire body, vibrating through his skull and into his mind. "Your dragon sleeps unprotected. The temple's barriers are not impervious to the right kind of power. Decide … Go to her when your affliction fades, or follow me and save your sister."

"Save her from what?"

But the man only stood and turned away.

"Don't you dare fucking hurt my sister! I'll hunt you down. I'll kill you, you bastard!"

The man let out a dark chuckle. "Good."

Naaz twisted his head to track the man's movements. He bent down over Neela's inert body, reached out an arm that seemed crafted of black opal, and brushed her hair off her cheek in an oddly tender gesture. Then he lifted her in his arms, cast one more look to Naaz, and in a blink disappeared like he'd never been there.

Naaz screamed in frustration. He tried to drift, but despite the skill being practically innate, it wouldn't work this close to the temple. If they could have drifted within a hundred miles of the place, he and Neela would have been there days ago. Yet that creature who had taken her had used a similar power to disappear.

He gave up yelling when his voice grew hoarse and he realized he couldn't move to reach his canteen, even to wet his lips.

Refocusing his attention inward, he found the burning

glow of Asha's energy that had been in his periphery for months, but had become his entire world for the past several weeks. She was so close. Barely another few hours of walking and he'd be at the temple ... He had to be that close.

But he had no idea where Neela could have been taken, not even a general direction in which to chase the man—the *creature*—who had taken her. What the hell did he want with her? If he was somehow under Meri's control, it could be bad, and those had definitely been Hunters they'd fought earlier.

But it would be worse if Naaz wasted valuable time chasing a ghost. Asha was out there waiting for him, and he knew exactly where she was. Better to head toward the dragon he knew how to find. With luck, she'd accept his worthless ass and at least help him save his sister from the beast who had taken her.

After about an hour staring up at the stars, his limbs began to tingle and he could move again. The world around him was quiet, confirmation that he was indeed within the range of a powerful dragon. They'd seen fewer and fewer signs of desert wildlife the closer they got to the temple. Humans were the only animals who risked venturing close to a dragon's lair. And cats ... For some strange reason, cats had no compunctions about being near dragons.

Arrogant little fuckers. What Naaz would have given to at least have a cat along for this solitary final leg of his trip.

CHAPTER 5

NEELA

The world swayed and tilted as Neela regained consciousness.

She glanced around and sat up, cautiously taking stock as her surroundings steadied. Something soft cushioned her from beneath, and she was covered in a comfortable, warm blanket. Everything else seemed the same. She was in her dirty trekking clothes, her knife still at her belt. Groping around in the shadows, she reached a dark lump and found her pack.

As her eyes adjusted, she could make out the walls of a cozy compartment not much larger than her old prison cell, though this one was made of smooth, curved stone that felt warm beneath her palm, and the bed she lay on was huge and luxurious. A slight air current filtered past, and she looked up to see a chimney-like passage extending vertically above her, opening up to a starry sky.

It was the strangest bed she'd ever seen, but that was all it was. No prison doors or bars caged her in, and though it was difficult to make out in the dim light, open space extended

"]

even farther beyond the bed, illuminated by the warm glow of lights coming from outside this chamber.

"Naaz?" she called in a low voice. "Brother, are you here?"

She heard no answer, and worse yet, she had no sense of her twin's nearness. The last thing she remembered was arguing with him about the direction they should go to reach the temple. He'd seemed so certain it was the other way, but her instincts had told her otherwise. She'd been following Zorion's power for days. She'd know whether she was going the right direction or not.

She shook her head. The subconscious flare of power that had led her forward wasn't where she remembered it. For so long, it had simply been like a lighthouse in the distance. A marker for her to follow whenever his dark presence wasn't beside her.

That power was all around her now. That meant he was *here*.

Her skin prickled with excitement, yet she had no sense of direction to lead her to him.

"Zorion, are you there?"

She crawled to the oblong opening at the side of the bed and slipped out, her bare feet hitting a warm stone floor. Glancing down, she found her boots and slipped into them. She headed in the direction of the light, reaching out with her mind and hoping for contact. He was here ... he had to be ... but this place, wherever she was, definitely was *not* a dragon temple.

The place was a warren of smooth pale ocher sandstone corridors, worn away in organic shapes, like some giant worm had carved its way through the bedrock over eons. What was left behind was a honeycomb of odd compartments about twice Neela's height, joined by corridors that were more like big, twisting tubes.

"Zorion, I know you're here. Please tell me where we are.

What happened to Naaz? Why aren't we in the temple?"

"Naaz must walk a separate path for now. My sister's happiness depends on it."

The voice was oddly formal and distant, nothing like the Zorion she remembered visiting her even as recently as the night before.

"Are you all right? Are you really *here*? If you're awake, I want to see you."

She tried to get a sense of his location from the pulses of power that surrounded her, but couldn't make sense of any of it. Short bursts came from one direction, so she turned and followed them, growing frustrated at every turn when she still failed to reach the source.

"I want to be with you. Please don't make me wait. Not after so long."

"Can you love darkness? Do you know of my origins? I am not light like my sister. I am a monster."

She'd never seen this broody side of him before. Every other time they'd communicated, he'd been all about protecting her, blocking her mind from the horrors of what they did to her in her Ultiori prison.

"That's bullshit. I *do* love you. And I want to see you. Why are you hiding from me?"

"To make you see."

"Nothing can be as dark as my own soul, baby. After what I've done, and what's been done to me, your presence is the only thing that makes me feel like I have any worth."

But after one last little burst of power, he was gone.

She locked onto that one glimmering pulse and headed in its direction. After a few more minutes of wandering, she reached an intimate room with a table in the center, incongruously set with a white tablecloth, shining silver, and china. Delicious scents wafted to her and her stomach growled.

God, real food would be ambrosia after a week of living on rationed trail mix, protein bars, and what sparse wildlife they could kill and roast. They'd brought enough food for a two-week trip, expecting to complete it in one, but that had taken more than two months.

She beelined to the table and sat, lifting the lid on the dish in the center. She didn't even bother serving herself from the platter—she just grabbed the entire dish and dug in, spearing a roasted chunk of meat and popping it into her mouth.

"Oh, you beautiful man, you definitely know the way to my heart." Spying a bottle of wine, Neela uncorked it and tilted it over the glass, deciding she could at least be civilized enough not to drink straight from the bottle. She took a big gulp to wash down the food and sighed, slowing down now that the hunger pains had dissipated and she could enjoy the meal properly.

There was even dessert, which was some decadent-looking thing made of frothy layers of cake and fresh fruit. A trifle, she thought it was called, though desserts weren't something she'd spent much time pondering. She'd been trapped in a cell for centuries with only the blandest food for nourishment, and hadn't exactly had time to enjoy the finer things since being released.

"I don't know if you're out there, but I sure hope you're at least enjoying this vicariously through me," she said to the empty room. "It would taste even better if I could share it with you, you know."

"I am enjoying your enjoyment, adara. Let me do this for you."

"What I want most is to see you," she said. "If all I wanted were tasty meals and soft beds, I didn't need to come all this way to find that. I want *you*."

The bright presence retreated again and Neela let out a curse. Why did he keep hiding?

CHAPTER 6

NEELA

There wasn't any kind of pattern to the network of chambers Neela explored after finishing the delicious meal. Some had skylights similar to the portal over the bed she'd awakened in. None had windows, however, which suggested this place was deep underground.

And yet she didn't find any stairways or ramps that led upward, despite searching repeatedly and retracing her steps several times. This place possessed the kind of power present within a dragon temple, but without the elaborate architecture. But someone had come back through and methodically carved little alcoves along all the walls, within which were placed small glowing orbs of dragon stone.

She rounded one arcing corridor and paused abruptly at the sound of voices carrying from several yards away. Male voices bantered, peppered with curses and laughter. They sounded friendly, at first, but with a tinge of the familiar that set her on edge. She leaned against the wall with her head tilted in the direction of the conversation, listening.

"Who cares what he wants her for? We did the job, we got paid."

"Fucking rather not have to get my throat slit to get paid, if it's all the same to you."

"You're alive, aren't you?"

"He's sending us back to fuck with the brother again soon. I've half a mind to cut the bastard again for this. Stabbed me in the fucking balls. I owe him. I don't care if the wound healed, I still felt the knife go in."

"Man, just do your fucking job. We don't want to cross this bastard any more than we'd have crossed Doctor Waters. I'm not sure which of them's the bigger psycho."

Doctor Waters? Neela's blood went cold. The familiar banter of mercenaries was clear now. Not just any mercenaries, either … These were probably the Ultiori Hunters who'd been tormenting them all along.

A voice carried closer and she shrank back, pressing her back to the wall.

"I'm getting a move on. We gotta be at the temple doors by the time the brother gets there. Can't make this fucker's job easy, can we?"

The brother … Her brother? Jesus Christ, who else could it be? Was Zorion somehow trapped under Meri's control with this group of Hunters standing guard? That would make sense … and explain why she and Naaz had been separated. Perhaps they'd been unable to capture him too, and he knew better than to chase them. He'd need Asha to fight these guys.

That didn't explain the delicious meal she'd stumbled across … or Zorion's evasiveness.

The voice came closer, and she tilted her head slightly to see. A figure clad in black fatigues came partway into view from an open doorway, his back to her as he paused to talk shit to the men still in the room. She could get answers if she played this right.

Hand on the hilt of her knife, she eased forward, drawing

on centuries of Hunter training to remain dead silent. She reached him, and with a swift kick to his legs and a blast of her last dregs of power to his neck, she had him on his knees with his head wrenched back and her knife to his throat.

"Tell me where the fuck you're keeping Zorion, or he dies."

Half a dozen men lurched to their feet, playing cards scattering on the table between them.

"Jesus fuck. He didn't say you'd be dangerous."

"You're goddamn right I'm dangerous. Tell me who's in charge and where the fuck you're holding the dragon."

The men darted confused glances between each other. The guy whose hair she had in a death grip swallowed and muttered, "I told you fucks we should've taken away her weapons."

"Honey, the dragon's the one paying us. Nobody's holding anyone."

"Bullshit. If he weren't a prisoner, he'd have come to me. Take me to him, or else."

They continued staring at her like imbeciles. "Lady, you don't know what the fuck you're talking about."

She wrenched harder on the Hunter's head and dragged the edge of her blade along his stubbled neck. He let out a strangled cry and tried to pull away as her knife sheared away part of his beard, but she held firm, keeping him paralyzed with just the barest hint of the Blue dragon magic left in her veins.

"Holy shit, what are you?" he yelped. "Nobody but a dragon or an Elite's stronger than one of us. And if you were a dragon, you'd have shifted."

"Come to think of it, they both fought like Hunters," one guy said. "Do you think they're the defectors?"

"Nah, women can't be Elites … can they?"

"Naaz is my brother. You know, the one you were just

threatening to maim a minute ago?" She dug her blade into the man's neck. Blood welled as the edge cut through skin. How could they not know that she and Naaz were the defectors?

"Jesus, we don't plan to kill him! Just … you know, make his job harder. Those were our orders. Make him work to get into the temple, then leave him to it."

He let out a yelp as her knife dug deeper. "Tell. Me. Where. He. Is."

"Lady, your brother's on his way to the temple."

"Not him! Zorion!" Her wrist twitched with the urge to simply slit the man's throat and be done with it.

Before she could give in, heat flooded the room, and her awareness was inundated with power strong enough to make every cell in her body vibrate. Her heartbeat sped up and desire shot through her.

A breath gusted across her ear as a big hand reached past her and landed over the fist that gripped the blade.

Smooth, velvet lips caressed the shell of her ear, Zorion's deep voice barely more than a whisper. "They don't lie, *adara*. They answer to me. Now please let this poor man go before he soils himself."

She remained frozen, heart pounding, breath caught in her throat as that slight brush of lips moved lower and pressed hotly at the side of her neck.

Molten heat shot through Neela's body. Time slowed down. In the scant few seconds Zorion's hand was in sight, her pulse beat hard through her veins, syncing to the steady, bright throb of light that emanated from the lines of fire that went through his big hand and up his arm. She barely had the presence of mind to look down as she released the blade and it clattered to the floor. He held her hand a second longer before retreating.

"Zorion. It's you!" She released her hold on the Hunter,

no longer caring about anything but the fact that her dragon had come. She turned to face him, but was met with only shadows and the tingling warmth of where his lips had brushed her skin only a moment ago.

"Come back!" she yelled into the corridor, but her voice only echoed back at her. She rubbed at the hot brand his mouth had left on her skin and turned around again, desperate now for answers. "Tell me where he is, please!"

The Hunters all stared back, then glanced at each other. The one who she'd been about to eviscerate rose to his feet and looked down at her. "He's our paycheck. That's all. We don't ask questions. He keeps us alive."

"But Meri … the Ultiori … How did you break free of Doctor Waters?"

"He had a better offer. It wasn't that tricky to decide."

Neela looked around the room at all of them, realizing it was pointless to argue. Hunters were often oblivious to how much control Meri had over their minds. Somehow Zorion had counteracted that control … but had he mind controlled them too?

She had so many questions now, but none of that mattered. She just needed to find him.

Giving up on the men in front of her, she turned and jogged down the corridor again, reaching out to grasp at whatever glimmer of a clue Zorion might have left as to his whereabouts.

"Why the hell do you keep running from me?" she asked the empty air, nearly in tears. No answer came, but she sensed another bright pulse of energy coming from the direction of the center of this odd underground compound. She followed it, the heat of his touch lingering on her skin.

CHAPTER 7

NAAZ

"Fucking hell, not again," Naaz grumbled when he came over a small rise and saw a group of Hunters waiting on the path ahead. They stood with arms crossed, five across, in front of a cliff that to any outside observer would have looked like a dead-end box canyon. Naaz knew better. The temple entry was beyond that red stone. On the other side of the wall of assholes determined to make his life miserable.

"Make it easy on yourselves and leave before I have to kill you!" he called. They simply straightened up and stared him down.

As he drew closer, he frowned. He was sure these were the same guys who had attacked them earlier and been slaughtered, yet they looked no worse for wear. In fact, they looked bright-eyed and ready to fight.

He sauntered forward, giving them a sardonic look, and stopped a few yards away with his hands on his hips, eyeing them. Yep, these were the very same men. Though one of them did apparently have an injury still, it couldn't be more than a flesh wound, judging from the bandage taped to the side of his neck.

Glancing at the man to his left, he grinned, recalling the particularly brutal attack he'd made on the guy's groin. "How's it hangin', friend?"

The man's already surly expression turned positively enraged. He dropped his hands, grabbed his blade, and launched himself at Naaz, spewing curses as he moved.

Naaz crouched, his muscles bunched as he readied to deflect the attack. The others only watched, seeming to bide their time until the first attacker was nearly beaten. Naaz didn't bother with a fatal blow this time, instead kicking the guy squarely in the groin before knocking him out with the pommel of his knife.

He rounded in time for the second man to come at him, blade drawn. He proceeded to subdue each of them in turn, all the while baffled by the methodical way they attacked. It was as if he'd accidentally walked into a training drill and they might wake up and try again at any second. Once all five men were down, he stared at their unconscious bodies.

"Whatever the fuck you guys are up to, I'm not about to let you get in my goddamn way again."

He traced a circle into the dirt with the heel of his boot and crouched down, drawing on the dragon power that remained in his blood. He exhaled a puff of red smoke, and with his fingertips directed it into a circle along the path he'd drawn. From there, he mentally commanded it into a shimmering red shield that surrounded the five Hunters. If they came to and breached the barrier, they'd be too overwhelmed by lust to remember they were after him and wander off to hunt for a quick lay.

He pressed his lips together in a grim line. The dragon blood that fueled his power was diminishing in his body. As one of the Ultiori Elites, he and his fellows had been given regular transfusions to keep them flush with power. The immortal blood was what had kept him and Marcus and Sterlyn alive for as long as it had. It was the power imbued by the Red dragon Gavra's blood that he'd used to soothe his female counterparts in the breeding experiments his former master had forced him to take part in. Even though the waning of that power made him vulnerable to attacks that otherwise wouldn't be fatal, he almost welcomed the idea of finally being at risk of dying in a fight.

Perhaps it would come to that, once he found the man who had taken his sister. If he had to fight to the death to ensure her survival, he would gladly do so. For now, he needed to get into the temple and reach Asha, and hope she had the power to help him.

At the bare rock face before him, he expelled another small breath, the smoke seeking out the telltale crevices of the stone lock. There were only two dragons within this temple, and either of their mates could trigger the catch to open the door.

The smoke trailed around in a circle, seeping through in a pattern that made Naaz's pulse throb in his ears. The red glow turned to ultraviolet, then bright white, and he pressed his palm to the center of the dragon-shaped glyph.

The cliff face heated beneath his hand, then stone grated against stone as the surface parted, revealing a dark corridor beyond.

His awareness of Asha's power grew, the bright pinprick of energy that had led him so far growing to a globe the size of the sun. Up until now, he'd only ever had the sense of her love and expectant longing for him, which he seriously doubted he could ever live up to.

But now ... now there was more.

"You're here! Oh, Sweet Mother, it's finally happening."

The lilting feminine voice was music to his ears. "Asha, is that really you, baby?" he said, breaking into a jog.

A laugh that reminded him of rain filtered into his mind. *"I like the sound of your voice. And I like you calling me that ... baby. Say it again."*

His throat constricted and he paused for a beat at the top of a wide spiral staircase that led down into darkness, the only light coming from the fire-imbued opal the walls were made of. He couldn't give her hope that he was the one. God, was he just going to use her, though? Saving his sister meant everything, but was it worth defiling this perfect pure light that had filled him with hope for so long?

"Baby ... we need to talk before I get to you."

"Uh oh. That sounds so serious. What's wrong?"

"I ... need your help. My sister was supposed to be with me."

"Yes! I know. Zorion has been beside himself over her arrival. Is she there too?"

"She's been captured. I need your help to save her after you're awakened."

"I will do anything you need me to do, my love. She is my family too. Or will be, especially once you and I are bonded, and she to my brother."

He reached the bottom of the staircase and emerged into a cavernous throne room. If Erika and the others' accounts of their own discovery held true, the hibernation chambers would be through doorways behind the throne. He spied the doors and ran for them, nearly falling flat when they opened smoothly with the barest touch of his hands.

Walking slowly, he approached the pair of huge doors within, each one crafted specifically with the chamber's occupant in mind. One door stood ominous in shining black, shot through with veins of multicolored fire. Beside this one was another, striking in its contrast and every bit as breathtaking. This door was pure, opaque white variegated with the same rainbow of flickering tendrils. Asha's door, and beyond it, she lay waiting for him to perform an act too vile for him to comprehend. He didn't know how he would complete this, only that he needed to, but he needed her to know the truth.

"Baby, I need to wake you up, because I need your help to find Neela. But you need to know that I'm really not the man for you. I … I've done things. Terrible things. If you turned me away now, I would get it. I'd make do. But please … before you take my advice and wait for someone better, help me find my sister."

He stood outside her door, staring at his feet with one hand raised. His palm itched to press against the surface, but he didn't want to start this if she told him to leave now.

Warmth enveloped his mind like a big, soft hug. *I'm not giving you up. Yes, I will help you, but because we belong together. I'll do it for my brother and for you, and for me too. Because I love you. Ever since you found me that first time and Papa hid me from you, I have dreamed about you. Papa told me how good you are, Naaz. He wouldn't lie to me.*

Naaz let out a shaky breath and shook his head. "I don't deserve you, Asha. Please think about it."

Why don't you get in here and wake me up, and we can talk about it face to face? I've waited for you forever! Stop wasting more time.

Feeling supremely guilty for even letting her talk him into going through with it, he pressed his palm to the door. Energy pulsed against his skin and the doors swung open, displaying an ornately decorated room.

In the very center of the room was a low oblong pedestal, upon which rested a sarcophagus Naaz would have known anywhere. And on the far side of the room opposite the door was a bed more luxurious than any he'd set eyes on. A fleeting image of making love to Asha, tangled among those silken sheets, passed through his mind just before he banished it. The bed would get no use. He would do what needed to be done to wake her, and nothing more.

But when he approached the sarcophagus, he faltered. It was the same ancient treasure Nikhil had hoarded away from him millennia ago. At the time, he'd had no idea what it was, or what needed to be done with it—only that it meant everything to him, and that he was willing to slaughter thousands in exchange for his master's allowance to even set eyes on the thing once more.

That had never happened, but now that he was here, he realized he had no idea what to do.

Before he and Neela had left Nikhil's army, they'd had an evening to talk with Erika and her team about their experiences awakening the current brood of dragons. Only the Court dragons had required the infusions of Nirvana that were fed to the Queen, who in turn channeled her power to the other dragons to end their hibernation. But in all their stories, the dragons had been merely frozen in their true shapes for the humans to touch and caress and make love to.

What lay before him was nothing like the true shape of a woman, or even a dragon. It was only a stylized representation of a female, shrouded in a white robe with a gilded headdress and painted eyes.

He walked to the side of the sarcophagus and brushed his fingertips over it. Though the stone was smooth, it was cold and uninviting.

"This can't be you ..."

Asha laughed. *"No, silly. I'm inside. Open it. Pretend I am a present for you and it's Christmas. I'd like to see what Christmas is like for real someday."*

His lips quirked at the innocent lilt of her voice, but it reminded him of how very inexperienced she was, despite the pair of them being only a few years apart in age. When you had lived more than three thousand years, a difference of three years meant nothing, yet he had done so many things in his long life … horrible things … while she had lain here, chaste and pristine.

He drew his hand back, hating himself for even thinking he could reveal her innocence to him. He abstractly wished the roles were reversed—that he could be one of the Guardians trapped in hibernation, waiting for the Virgin to claim him.

"We can pretend you're a statue and I'm a virgin, if you want. After you wake me up, though—if it will make you feel better."

Naaz let out a sigh. "I'm not sure anything will make me feel better about what I'm about to do."

He slipped his fingertips beneath the edge of the sarcophagus and lifted, hooking his hands around the heavy carved stone lip to gain better leverage. With all his strength, he hoisted the stone likeness of the woman up and heaved it off the other side. The cover smashed against the floor in a resounding thud, cracking into pieces on contact.

His breath caught in his throat at the sight before him. Asha's pale skin was marbled with prismatic fire. Her shape was perfection, from the pure white silk of her hair and her full, ripe breasts with her hands folded above them in the center of her chest, to her tiny navel. His gaze skittered past the juncture of her thighs, refusing to dwell too long on the smooth skin and tickling thoughts of what lay between— how she might taste, how she might feel.

The warmth of her hit him then, startling him into action. It couldn't be … Despite the inhuman coloring of her skin, she had a glow that was contrary to what he'd expect from a hibernating dragon. From all the accounts he'd heard, they were indistinguishable from statues, as hard and solid as stone. Yet Asha looked real, and when he ventured a shaky hand to reach out and touch her cheek, he drew back in alarm as if she'd shocked him.

"*What is it, my love?*" she asked.

"Your body isn't stone. It's flesh. Oh, fuck. I can't do this. I won't … do *this* to you."

"*Do what? All you need is to give me your Nirvana. Is it hard to do for you?*"

Naaz let out a bitter laugh. "Oh, baby, that's never been hard for me. My filthy dick has a one-track mind, and *it* certainly wants you. But you can't move, and somehow I'm expected to make love to you like this. I just can't do it."

CHAPTER 8

NEELA

The beacon lured Neela into yet another room where a surprise awaited, but Zorion himself was nowhere to be found. Fragrant steam wafted from the room, concealed only by a gauzy curtain blocking the path. When she passed through, her breath caught at the magical sight. Candle flames flickered from small ledges carved into the walls, and from around the edges of a sunken bath wide enough for several people to lounge without touching.

Neela wandered to the edge and crouched, dipping her fingers into the hot water. Her aching muscles responded to the prospect of a relaxing bath by screaming their reminder of how long and arduous a trip she'd taken to get here. But the merry chase Zorion was leading her on was starting to make a little sense now.

"Sweetie, if you wanted to get me naked, all you had to do was ask."

A faint shadow seemed to travel around the room, causing all the flames to quiver and the hair on her nape to stand on end. She raised her hand to rub at the still tingling spot where he'd kissed her neck.

If this was what he needed to show himself, then she'd happily do it.

"I don't know what your deal is. If it's my B.O. that's keeping you away, you could've said so."

She kicked off her dusty boots and undressed, taking her time and making a show of it, sure he must be observing from the shadows somehow. He could *be* a Shadow, for all she knew. His father was none other than the Void himself, but she knew a dragon's colors and its very nature were determined by the relationship its parents had more than genetics. There was no telling what Zorion's true nature was, but that brief glimpse she'd had of him suggested something more unique than she'd ever imagined. Clearly he need a little encouragement, though, if she wanted to see him face-to-face.

Naked, she dipped a toe into the hot pool and gingerly stepped in, striding down the steps that led into the water. The steam was scented of night-blooming flowers, and she inhaled deeply, letting the heat seep in to relax her tired, grimy body.

"You do know how to pamper a girl, I'll give you that," she said, floating onto her back and letting herself drift on the surface with her eyes closed.

She floated like that for several moments, letting her limbs go lax and studiously ignoring her irritation that he persisted in avoiding her.

A soft draft filtered through, cooling her exposed skin. Only the tips of her breasts, her face, and her knees remained above the surface, and the air seemed to dance over her. She sighed, imagining the air was his breath, blowing on her nipples and teasing them to hard peaks.

The room darkened beyond her closed eyelids, and she opened them. She stood up, alarmed at first by the utter blackness that surrounded her, until she caught a glimpse of flickering color on the far side of the pool where she'd entered.

What she saw was a surreal, glowing shape of a man who seemed to be crafted of multicolored fire that twined around his body in a network of effulgent tendrils. She could make out no features other than the size and shape of him. Large, with broad shoulders and a thickly muscled torso. The displacement of the water was the only sign that he had actual mass and wasn't just made of a strange mix of darkness and fire.

She blinked several times, worried that he might be a mirage—some trick of her tired eyes and her need to finally see him. Not that she could see much in the darkness, but what she *could* see enthralled her.

Her throat tightened and she struggled to swallow past the knot in it when he reached her. He was so tall she had to crane her neck to look into the iridescent orbs that swirled where his eyes should be.

"Do I frighten you?"

She blinked, disoriented by the way his voice seemed to fill the air from all sides, as well as echo inside her mind.

"No. My god, is that really you?"

She took an impulsive step toward him and reached out. He flinched back and grabbed her hand in his. Neela's heart stopped at the sudden, unexpected force of that contact, the squeeze of his hand around hers and the soft caress of his thumb in the center of her palm. He tilted his head to the side and directed his ethereal gaze to her hand, exploring the center in little circles with his thumb before meeting her eyes again.

Her heartbeat synced with the pulsing light emanating from beneath his strange, dark skin. Heat built in the water between them, the air growing even thicker with steam. It solidified around her, pushing at her back, but she needed little urging to close the distance.

It was as though a rough tide surged behind her, but it could have come from within. Either way, she launched into his arms like she'd been pulled into a well of gravity too strong for her to possibly resist.

"Neela," he growled as his arms closed around her. "*Adara*, I'm not ready for you, but I had to see you, touch you, taste you, to believe you were really here and not another waking dream."

He brought his hands up to her face, which warmed under the glow of his eyes. His thumbs traced her brows, and she let her eyelids fall shut as he brushed the pads over the soft skin to her cheeks, then down. He caressed her lips, and they parted. She darted her tongue out, mouth watering for more intimate contact, and he obliged, slipping the tip of his thumb inside. She sucked, letting out a soft moan of need, her core tightening with desire.

With a single, swift scoop, he hoisted her higher, hooking one arm beneath her ass as she wrapped her legs around his torso. Their faces drew level, and one molten glance passed between them before their lips touched and their mouths merged.

Neela clung to him through the kiss, overwhelmed by the sensation of heat and softness and pure desire that washed through her. Never in her life had any male incited this kind of all-consuming fire in her.

He brushed his free hand up her side and cupped her cheek as his tongue swept deep, ravenously tasting her. She moaned into his mouth, tightening her grip on him. God, she wanted to climb inside his skin and live there forever. The light raking of nails down her side suggested he wanted the same thing, and he left trails of pure fire along her skin before slipping his hand between them to cup her breast.

He found her nipple and pinched it lightly, the sharp sensation sending a bolt of pleasure like an earthquake rending her body in two. She cried out, tilting her head back and arching into him. His hot mouth replaced his fingers, his lips and teeth plucking at the taut flesh, flooding her core with even more wet heat.

She bucked against him, craving more contact, but this wasn't enough.

"I need to see you. My whole life, you've always come to me in shadows. Please let me see you for real now."

"Need you," he growled, sucking harder on her nipple and slipping the hand that held her backside down until his fingers grazed her spread opening.

The contact set off white-hot blasts of heat in her brain, her body tensing on the very edge of what might be the quickest climax of her life. She struggled to tamp it down, because she wanted more—wanted this first moment with him to be more than just two bodies writhing in the darkness.

"Stop!" She smacked her hands against his shoulders, pushing him away.

He pulled back, his glowing eyes flashing beneath fluttering eyelids. His breath came in quick, rough pants, betraying his own barely contained desire.

"We are bound. Fated since time began. Why are you fighting this?"

"I'm not ... Fuck, I want you, but not like this. Not in the dark with my imagination having to fill in the blanks. In the dark you might as well be some other man ..."

"It is me ... Zorion ..."

Something wavered in his voice and she pushed harder, prying herself out of his arms and barely catching herself as he relented, releasing her back into the water. "Why don't you sound convinced of that yourself? What are you keeping from me?"

All the churning confusion of the past few hours tangled into a writhing knot in her chest and she backed away. "How are you even here? I thought … I thought I had to make love to you in the temple to even wake you up."

"I'm not like other dragons, Neela. The first temple you found me in all those ages ago was enough to contain my power. The temporal bubble Asha's father kept us in blocked all but our barest mental link. But the new temple was easy for me to breach with my fire."

"Are you a Shadow? I've never seen anything like you, but I want to see you in the light."

"I am more … more than my mother and father combined. A piece of the Mother Dragon was made whole when they joined and made me. But it isn't a pretty piece. I think I must be made of the darkest parts of them. I am the product of the unholiest union, unlike my sister, who was conceived from the purest form of love … that of a man willing to sacrifice his very soul for his lover's happiness."

"You think that because your parents were siblings, that makes you somehow unholy? I beg to differ. You were always there for me, Z. You kept the darkness from eating me alive. I only wish you could have done the same for my brother. He didn't have the blessing of such a connection with Asha. Not even his dreams of her could keep him from the taint of what they did to us. *You* protected me from all that, so as far as I'm concerned, you're a fucking angel. Please let me see you."

"I am trying to help your brother as we speak. He will be made whole soon enough."

"Where is he now?"

"He is with Asha. He fights to protect her from himself, but is willing to give up love to protect you from me. I wasn't sure if he would be worthy of my sister if he couldn't see his own value, but I've changed my mind. I think being with her will make him worthy. Asha can be convincing."

Neela's brow twitched at the deep affection and humor in his voice. He reminded her of Naaz, with his quiet tolerance of his sister's quirks.

"He's all right, then? The Hunters ... or whoever they are ... were talking about attacking him earlier."

"They were a ruse, simply meant to give him a reason to fight. Taking you was part of that."

"Wait, were *you* behind all the ambushes we've fought off all this time? And I guess taking me was only meant to torture my brother, is that right?" She crossed her arms over her bare breasts and lifted an eyebrow at the glowing eyes that regarded her.

"I didn't say that. You belong with me, *adara*. Torturing my sister's future mate was a bonus."

She growled low in her throat, trying to decide whether she despised this man or loved him more for his irreverence.

"Well, you can stop now. I want you to let him know I'm all right."

"It's a little late for that." When she lifted her eyebrows again, he let out a sigh that made the air shimmer between them. "All right. Follow me, and you can at least see him. If you still want me to contact him, I will."

He turned away, but rather than stride out of the pool like a normal man, he simply disappeared.

"Jesus fucking Christ, why can't I drift in here?"

"It isn't drifting. There's no displacement of time. My fire simply travels more quickly than your human senses can track. Come to me, adara."

With a soft whoosh of air, all the candles relit. Neela waded out of the pool and found a pile of clean towels folded neatly on a ledge nearby. Her core still ached with unquenched need, but she ignored it and found her clothes.

Whatever kept Zorion from showing himself would have to give. As much as she wanted him, she couldn't stand the idea of making love to him without being able to look into his eyes. His *real* eyes, not those strange fiery orbs he kept showing her in the darkness.

She dressed again and followed the pulsing beacon that broadcast his location. Again, he led her through a tangled maze of twisting corridors that left her completely turned around. She entered another room, this time lit with dragon globes mounted on the walls like bright sconces. Zorion was nowhere to be seen, but she could sense him in the shadows.

"Move to the reflecting basin," he commanded, the timbre of his voice sending a pleasant shiver down her spine. She could listen to him talk forever and never get tired of the sound.

She stepped to the center of the room where a sandstone pedestal rose out of the floor with a concave depression worn into its surface. Before her eyes, the well filled with water. The ripples evened out, leaving the surface mirror-smooth, and within the reflected depths, something more detailed than the nondescript reflection of the ceiling above her came into view.

CHAPTER 9

NAAZ

*N*aaz clenched his fists at his sides, agonizing over the sight before him.

"It is me, my love. I am only in stasis. My mind is awake, yet my body cannot move until you revive it."

"I won't fuck you like this, Asha. Please don't ask me to do that."

"Then don't. I only need your Nirvana."

Naaz let out a snort. "As if me jacking off is any better? I want our first time to be … special. Not just some pointless grasping for pleasure on my part. I want you to love it."

"Then make love to me as if I were awake. Trust my voice. Tell me what you would do first."

He took a deep breath and moved to the head of her pedestal. "I would kiss you," he said, his voice rough. "God, that's all I've been able to think of since the dreams began. The way it feels to kiss you."

"Do you not make love to me in the dreams?"

"No … because my cock isn't good at making love. Great at fucking … not the kind of thing you deserve."

"Have you ever tried making love before?"

He thought back to the one time he'd had the chance to. But Evie hadn't wanted to be made love to, which he understood completely now. Marcus and Ked were the only men who should be allowed to make love to Evie. Just as Asha was the only woman for Naaz.

"Once … I tried it once with a friend, but it didn't work out. I want it to work this time."

"Does that mean you will stay with me after?"

"God, Asha. I don't know. I want you so fucking much. It tears me up to think of how wrong I am for you."

"How will you know if you're wrong, unless you try?"

He swallowed thickly, gazing down at the perfect, serene beauty that lay before him. Her lips were a sweet, pink bow, perfect for kissing. Despite centuries of experience, he suddenly felt out of his element. His heart pounded so hard the thuds reverberated inside his skull as he lowered his face to hers.

When he pressed his mouth against her lips, he had the most surreal, fervent hope that somehow a kiss would be enough. That this would be the end of their perfect fairy tale, in which he braved the tangled, perilous obstacles keeping him from the princess, and that this kiss was the last step before their happily ever after.

But he was no prince, and while Asha was arguably the most beautiful, slumbering princess in existence, he knew the kiss was only the beginning.

Her voice was like a sigh inside his mind, a soft "oh" of wonder as though she'd just had some revelation about the nature of the universe. It spurred him on and he rested his palm against her pale cheek, brushing his thumb over her cheekbone as he tilted his head and deepened the kiss. Swiping his tongue between, he was met with the hard, unmoving barrier of her teeth and jolted back.

"Fuck. I don't know about this." Her lack of physical

response made it all too similar to the times he'd tried to deepen a connection with the females he'd been forced to couple with. He'd only sought to make the experience less horrifying.

"I liked it. I wish I could kiss you back. Once I'm awake, I think I will spend every spare moment kissing you."

"I liked it too. You're so soft." He impulsively reached out and brushed his fingertips over her cheek again, grazing his thumb across her lower lip. "Can you feel this?"

"Yes. I feel your heat near me. Your palm is a little rough. Is that how men feel?"

"Men who fight. These hands aren't used to making love, baby. You're bound to be disappointed."

"Do I feel good to you?"

He smoothed his palm over her shoulder and squeezed, marveling at how solid she was—how warm and *human*. She looked far more delicate than she felt.

"You feel amazing. I could do nothing but touch you all day and never get tired of it."

"Then touch me. Kiss me everywhere but my lips, so it doesn't scare you that I can't kiss back. When your hand is on me, it warms me from the inside in a way I've never felt before. Do you feel the same way?"

"Mmm ... warm, yes." He didn't elaborate, but touching her made his blood run hot and his dick throb almost painfully within the confines of his cargo shorts. He ignored the tightness, forcing himself to focus on her and only her. She evidently enjoyed his touch, and as long as he could incite those pleased little mental moans from her, he would keep trying.

"I'm going to kiss you some more, all right Asha?"

"Yes." Her voice sounded breathy and expectant. The mental image he had of her responded to the barest brush of his fingers along her collarbone with an arch of her neck to

give him better access. He traced a line down her sternum and paused, letting his big hand rest gently over hers where they lay folded over each other in the center of her chest, her forearms partially concealing her breasts from view. He bent and pressed a soft kiss at the hollow of her clavicle, then impulsively darted out his tongue.

"Do I taste good?" she asked.

"Like sunlight," he murmured, brushing his lips along the line of her shoulder.

Another mental sigh urged him on. He closed his hands over both of hers and lifted them off her chest, closing his eyes for a second to brace himself for the sight of her bare breasts. With deliberate care, he placed her hands at her sides and stood upright, letting his gaze drift over her, trying and failing to numb himself to her beauty. Her breasts were small but perfect, their weight only partially succumbing to gravity, the swell of one side casting a shadow over her ribcage.

"Where did you go? Naaz?" She sounded almost frantic, and he gripped her nearest hand in his and squeezed.

"I'm here, baby. I just … got a little overwhelmed there for a second."

"Do you like the way I look?"

"God, yes. You are a feast for sore eyes. I just had to take a moment to enjoy the sight."

"Oh, good. I worried when Zorion kept going on about how no human could ever love a creature as monstrous as he. He's my brother, so I must resemble him in some way, but if my appearance pleases you …"

"If your brother is anywhere close to as beautiful as you, Neela will adore him. But I think she'd adore him regardless. If it weren't for him, she'd be as messed up in the head as I am."

"You're not messed up. You're as kind and gentle as I hoped you would be. I wish you would kiss me again."

"There is nothing kind and gentle about the thoughts going through my head. Do you have any idea how badly I want to be inside you? Every image is of me defiling your perfect … innocence. Fuck, I am such a monster for letting that out."

"But you aren't doing that. You're doing what I asked. You're a good person."

"You don't understand. This is about power. You are helpless even though you can speak. You're naked and vulnerable, and I'm … a lot bigger than you, and practically wearing armor compared to you. Nothing about this situation is balanced in the least. I would rather be the one lying there with you molesting me."

"I would like that. But we can't try it until I'm awake. Why don't you just take your clothes off?"

Naaz almost objected. Being naked would have just made him feel more like a deviant sexual predator. But she had a point. If it was about power, removing his clothes would take some of that power away from him.

"All right. You win. I'll get naked for you."

He bent down to unlace his boots and kick them off, then peeled his shirt over his head. Red dust clouded the air, and he realized how very filthy he was. There was nothing to be done about that issue now, but his griminess somehow made him feel better when he stood beside her pristine body, clad in nothing but the dirt of his travels.

That's what his past was, after all. A fucking ordeal that had tarnished his very soul the same way the red dust of the godforsaken wasteland outside coated his skin. Somehow being naked beside such a perfect example of purity made that darkness feel superficial … If he could love a creature as flawless and genuine as Asha, didn't that make him a better person?

"I'm afraid to touch you now ... I'm kind of a mess. I'll get you dirty."

"Can I try something? I want to test my magic. See if I can make this work. I've never had someone close enough to try with, and my breath never made it out of the sarcophagus before."

"Anything you wish."

"Stand close to my head."

He moved to the end of the pedestal again, standing as close as he dared. This left less than a foot between his groin and Asha's lovely profile. He instinctively covered his erection, as though its presence might offend her.

"I'm here."

As he gazed down at her, shimmering iridescent smoke began to seep from her nostrils and the corners of her mouth, as if some small fire had been lit inside her and was starting to burn. The smoke floated around her head like a halo, and he could sense some effort going on from the little whispers of encouragement she emitted inside his mind. It was endearing ... as though she were trying to coax a small animal into doing a trick.

The smoke grew thicker and changed direction. He forced himself to hold still as the tendrils crept to the edge of the pedestal and floated farther, reaching out into the air where he stood, like fingers grasping for purchase on something.

"There you are!" she exclaimed when the first soft tine of smoke grazed his hand over his crotch.

The smoke flooded over him then, billowing in denser clouds from her nose and mouth until he was completely engulfed in a shimmering prismatic cloud. His skin tingled at the contact and he closed his eyes, swallowing the knot of emotion that choked him.

"This will work best if you breathe, my love," she said.

Naaz inhaled, the very act of deliberately expanding his

lungs helping ease the ache of this strange transformation that she seemed to have triggered in his very soul. The cloud of magic flowed around him, swirling in eddies against his skin, around his hands and arms. Up over his shoulders and down his back, the smoke carried away all the dust and grime of his travels and left behind nothing but his raw, aching hope that he could somehow be worthy of the woman who saw fit to give him this gift.

"Now you're all clean," she announced in a pleased voice moments later.

Naaz struggled to regain control of his voice. His eyes burned as he lifted his arms and gazed at them, then down his body at the complete lack of any sign of his journey. But better than that, he felt scrubbed clean on the inside, his every regret washed away in the flood of what he could only describe as *forgiveness* that had filled him.

He was left with the overwhelming need to be near her. Not desire, but something far deeper.

"Asha," he choked out when he could finally speak again. "I need to hold you."

"Yes," was all she said.

He eyed the pedestal and found the hard surface too uninviting for what he had in mind. He leaned down and slipped his arms beneath her shoulders and knees, lifting her and cradling her against his chest. His heart pounded at the closeness of all her soft skin.

"Where are you taking me?"

"To bed, baby. Where I can hold you and make love to you like I mean it."

The bed was a huge construction with elaborate, twisting columns of carved stone that held fire beneath its surface, much the way Asha's skin seemed to glow from within. The bedding was the softest down-filled mattress with luxurious silk sheets. Naaz was sure he'd sunk into a cloud when he climbed on and lay Asha down against the fluffy pillows.

He slipped down beside her, still cradling her against his chest and marveling at how small she felt compared to the way she completely owned his every thought.

When he settled with her head resting on his upper arm, he bent and pressed another brief kiss to her lips.

"Thank you," he said. "Now it's my turn to make you tingle all over."

"This feels good already. Your body against mine … I like how you're both hard and soft."

He glanced down between them at the stiff thickness of his shaft resting on the curve of her hip. The contact itself made him ache for more, but this had to be about *her* pleasure first.

"Ignore my dick. I can't help myself, being this close to you."

"Is that the part that's so hot against my hip? I feel the core of your power soaking through my skin right there. It makes me feel even more alive. I want more of that."

"You can have all of me after you're awake. For now, I want to make sure you know how good you can feel. Like this …"

He shifted his arm out from under her and rose up, propping himself above her with his free hand resting on her chest. Slowly he began to draw it downward, caressing between her breasts, around her ribcage, then up again to cup her breast and graze his thumb over her nipple. The small bud tightened and pebbled against his skin, and Asha let out a mental sigh that sent a pleasant shiver down his spine to settle into his cock.

"I want more like that," she said.

"Good, because I have more." He toyed with her nipple, tracing the pale pink circle of her areola until she panted inside his head and errant wisps of smoke escaped her mouth and nose. Then he switched to the other breast and teased until its tip was also flushed, bright and hard as a ripe cherry.

His mouth watered and he gave into the craving, dipping his head to take one bud into his mouth and suck.

"Oh, yes. Please kiss me like that everywhere."

Naaz couldn't help but let out a hungry growl as he opened his mouth and took in more of her breast, swirling his tongue around the supple flesh and grazing his teeth across her nipple until the sweet sounds she made drove him wild.

Feverish for more, he rose and swung his leg over her to straddle her. He cupped her breasts, pushing them together and bent again, teasing both nipples in quick succession while her presence squirmed inside his mind.

Soft heat soaked into his balls and he twitched, flinching as he realized he'd forgotten how naked he was. He hadn't meant to let his cock brush that close to her core, which he realized now was radiating heat.

"Why do you pull away?" she asked.

"Not ready to go that far yet. My cock can't have you until after I make you come."

"Let me feel it. Please. The magic soaks into my skin when you touch me with it. It makes my soul feel alive. The deepest parts of me sing with want."

"This turns you on?" he asked, leaning back on his haunches and lowering his ass until his skin met hers again and his balls rested just beneath her navel. His cock was a thick, rigid pole, and he gripped it and pushed down until it lay along the center of her belly like a slumbering snake.

"I feel ... swollen. Like I'm about to burst out of my skin if you touch me more. But that's what I want. I want you to kiss me and touch me until I catch fire and come to life again for real. Touch me with your tongue, with your hands, with your cock."

"Your wish is my command," he said, and bent again to take one nipple in his mouth, this time deliberately allowing his cock to slide against her skin, tilting his hips to give her the friction she seemed to want. His balls grazed over the top of her bare mound, and he was acutely conscious of the swell of her thighs and the heat coming from their apex.

He encountered warm wetness and paused, his eyelids fluttering closed at the realization that she wasn't simply responding to him in mental whispers and sighs, but that her body indeed reacted to the pleasure he was giving her.

He traveled lower, his head pounding with the barely checked desire to push her thighs wide and slide into that damp heat. He slowed long enough to savor the sensation of her crease parting slightly under the pressure of his cock. Beneath the sensitive head of his shaft, her tiny clitoris beat a steady pulse, reminding him how very alive she was and how strongly she desired what he hoped to give her.

"You can be inside me. It's what you wish, and I wish for it too."

"Not yet baby. Not until I can look into your eyes while you ride me."

"What will you do until then?"

"Keep making you wet like this."

Naaz forced his cock past the temptation of her sweet snatch and kissed his way down her belly. He pushed his knees between her legs, spreading her open, then sat back again to enjoy the sight before him. She was still serene and beautiful, as though she merely slept, but a slight pink flush now betrayed the level of desire that filled her. Her breathing was quicker, more tendrils of smoke steadily threading their way from her nose and mouth. If he didn't know better, he'd think she was simply faking sleep and playing some demented little game to make him do all the work.

He was happy to comply.

The glistening pink of her pussy spread wider as he

pushed her knees farther apart. Her scent brought back memories of night blooming jasmine that grew in the gardens outside the palace where he'd been born. The aroma reminded him that Asha had been conceived in that very palace not long after his own birth. What could their lives have been, if the vile creature who'd been his master had never existed? Would they have been raised together from the start, the daughter of a goddess matched to one of her godchildren?

He lay down between her legs, pushing her thighs up until her knees bent and her legs splayed, supported by his arms when he hooked them around her thighs. The breathy sound of his name filled his mind when his lips brushed over her slick folds and his eyes closed to let the scent wash over him fully. Even though her voice was still only in his head, he imagined she spoke it aloud, urging him to pleasure her.

Even if he'd only been a slave like his parents were to Belah then, he'd have happily been Asha's slave. With the first gentle graze of his tongue up the seam of her pussy, he let himself imagine they were back in that palace. That none of the past three thousand years had happened, and this moment was their first experience—the awakening that had been denied them by the beast he'd called a master.

He closed his mouth over her delicious, smooth folds, sinking his tongue deep into her luscious juices. He was determined that this would be the beginning of the two of them making up for not having had those three millennia together.

Her body's reactions were enough to urge him on. As he teased at her clit with his tongue, her petals grew soaked, and he licked the sweet ambrosia of her nectar away, reveling in the way she sang his name inside his head. He doubted *her* orgasm was what would wake her; he'd learned from the others that the human mate's Nirvana was the key, but his cock wept, and the sensation of the soft sheets beneath his hips made him reflexively thrust into the silken fabric.

All his senses were inundated with Asha, the slick velvet of her core beneath his mouth, the sweet flavor of her juices on his tongue. She made no sounds for him to hear, but the cries inside his head grew louder and louder. To be the man to drive this perfect, untouched angel to such mad desire was intoxicating, and he redoubled his efforts to push her higher.

Her flesh quivered and pulsed beneath his mouth and he slipped a finger into her opening, aching to feel her tight channel around part of him. He wasn't disappointed, especially when she moaned a desperate, *"Yes! More!"* that encouraged him to push another finger in and fuck her with them both. She clenched around him, a surprisingly strong, deliberate movement that was at odds with her otherwise placid body, but he only had a split-second to wonder at the movement before his mind split wide with the piercing cry of her orgasm.

Wetness flooded his mouth, along with a bright surge of pure power the likes of which he'd never experienced. He'd been a whore or a stud his entire life and was no stranger to the flood of magic when a dragon climaxed, but Asha's magic was pure white fire. It shot through him, searing away everything but the knowledge of his desperate love for her. And before he could control his reaction, his hips bucked into the bed, the friction against his cock providing just enough pleasure on top of the overwhelming rush for him to come harder than he ever had.

He didn't let himself stop to enjoy the moment, dead set on drawing out her pleasure for as long as possible. It wasn't until a pair of hands gripped his head and pulled him away that he realized what had happened.

He lifted himself up in a daze, blinking down at the lovely creature beneath him. Strange iridescent eyes like mother-of-pearl gazed back, framed by long lashes that blinked slowly up at him.

"Hi," he said, his mouth quirking into a smile.

"Hi back," she replied, then launched herself into his arms, barreling him over with a laugh.

He found himself pinned by unexpectedly strong hands. She peppered his face with kisses, her lithe body rubbing delightfully against his, making his flagging cock fully hard again.

"No moving!" she said when he struggled to pull from her grasp.

He laughed and lay still. "As you wish."

"It's your wish. You lay there, and I molest you. It's my turn."

"As long as that means I get to be inside you now."

"Oh, that's exactly what it means."

She rested her hands on his chest and pushed up, her hair a tangled mess as she stared down at him in utter wonder. Without speaking, she raised her hips and tilted forward until his tip slipped between her slick folds. The heat of that contact made him groan.

"I want to touch you ..." he said, but was halted by the press of her mouth against his and her tongue plunging between his lips. *This* was he kiss he'd hoped for, the one he'd dreamed of for so long, and he groaned and tilted his head up to kiss her back.

At the same time, she pushed down onto his cock, letting out a whimper as her tight sheathe accommodated his thick shaft. And then she was riding him, not like the chaste virgin he'd expected, but like the wild, powerful dragon he knew she really was. And he wouldn't change a fucking thing.

CHAPTER 10

NEELA

eela interrupted the scene in the reflecting pool with a puff of breath just as her brother lifted Asha's sleeping body and made his way to the bed. She bit down hard on her lower lip to stave off the sudden surge of pride and elation. Naaz would be all right. And to think he was on the verge of turning around and leaving not long before the last ambush …

The surface of the water cleared to mirror smooth again, but she kept staring at her own reflection, trying to decide if *she* might somehow be lacking. Perhaps she needed to find her own self-worth before Zorion would show himself to her.

But that made no sense. She was ready for him. She'd bared herself already. He was the one holding back, and she wasn't sure why.

Candlelight flickered in the reflection, revealing the rough-hewn red stone of the cave's ceiling. She narrowed her eyes and tilted her head, feigning interest in the surface as though she were still watching her brother's drama play out. She had an idea.

She gripped the edge of the basin and leaned closer, deliberately widening her eyes. "Z! Something's happening! Come look!"

Her back instantly warmed from his proximity and she resisted the urge to close her eyes and lean back against him. She kept her gaze fixed on the water and waited.

Sure enough, the shadow behind her soon coalesced and grew solid. Iridescent eyes glowed from within an ebony face shot through with a web of fiery light. Her heart nearly stopped at the beauty of his reflection, a sight as divinely perfect as the Milky Way had been all those nights painted in the night sky above the Outback. She saw eternity in his eyes, and wanted to let herself fall into it and never leave.

"I see nothing," he said, his coal-black brows drawing together. Then time stopped as his eyes met hers in the reflection. Alarm filled his gaze, and in a split-second, he disappeared just as quickly as he'd appeared. Too late, Neela realized that she'd been staring wide-eyed with her mouth hanging open. She cursed at herself. She'd probably looked like she was paralyzed with fear.

"Z, goddammit, I'm not afraid of you!" she yelled at the empty air. The ache of frustration inside softened a little in sympathy. In a softer voice, she said, "You're the most beautiful thing I've ever seen."

She sensed no telltale brightness in power revealing where he was, but wandered down the winding tunnels anyway, hoping she'd find some sign. Eventually she found her way back to the makeshift break room for the Hunters who apparently served Zorion now. The men were different than the ones she'd seen earlier, but gave her wary looks nonetheless.

She wandered on and found the barracks, which was a room similar to the one she'd awakened in, with cozy alcoves cut into the walls in tiers acting as bunks.

Several of the beds were occupied with large, vaguely man-shaped lumps. One Hunter was still awake. He stood looking into a small shard of mirror propped on a ledge near a waterfall trickling from a crack in the rock into a rough basin cut into the wall. He had remnants of shaving cream on his cheek, head tilted as he fiddled with something against his neck.

"I can help," she said in a low voice, making him jump and curse.

He narrowed his eyes. "You're the fucking cause. No thank you."

"I am sorry about that. I didn't know you worked for him. I see Hunters and I think 'enemy.'"

She took a cautious step closer and reached out a hand. "That poor excuse for a mirror isn't doing you any good. You need another set of eyes. Let me see."

He gave her another dark look and reluctantly turned, tilting his head to bare the side of his neck. Neela winced at the gash that ran across the underside of his jaw. She'd been aiming for his jugular and was right on the mark. Had she cut any deeper, he'd have bled out.

She gave him another apologetic look and he pressed his lips together.

"I thought he healed you," she said.

"Only fatal wounds or anything that keeps us from doing our jobs. This is a scratch. I can deal."

"Here, let me …" She reached for the fresh bandage and ointment he held in his hand. He reluctantly handed it to her and she stepped forward to take it.

He was a head taller than her, which put her at eye level with the wound. It really wasn't that terrible, but no doubt it hurt like hell. She opened the tube of ointment and squeezed a bit onto her finger, then gingerly dabbed it along the cut.

"What's your name?"

"Paolo," he said, still eyeing her warily, but holding still.

"I'm Neela."

"Yeah, we figured that out. Nobody but an Elite could've done what you did. You're a legend, you know? One of only two female Elites in the Ultiori. We thought you were both dead."

"One of us *is* dead," she said, her stomach clenching at the memory of a woman she'd once loved like a sister. Her skin prickled at the realization of how interconnected all their lives had been. Benedetta had nearly defected for the love of a dragon, but had been driven mad before she'd had a chance by the darkness that corrupted her mind.

Naaz and Neela had been there that day, had tried to control their friend's bloodlust. Neela herself had seen how far gone her friend was, and even tried putting her down herself, something she'd known she would regret for her entire life—but nothing could kill an Elite at full power, save the fire of the dragon whose blood gave her that power. In Benedetta's case, it was the very same dragon she'd loved before she'd gone insane.

Benedetta had been on an unsanctioned rampage, killing every dragon she encountered in her search for her lover. Neela and her brother had followed, and were there when she finally reached her target. Neela still didn't know exactly what had happened in those last few moments, only that Ked had taken Benedetta in his arms and breathed a cloud of thick black smoke around them. When it cleared, his eyes were filled with such anguish, Neela's heart broke. That was when he'd transformed into a huge black dragon and set his lover on fire.

"Where the hell have you been all this time?" Paolo asked. "I always heard there could only be three Elites. Did Marcus die?"

His voice cracked, and it reminded her that these men,

mercenaries though they were, were still humans and still had feelings when Meri wasn't in control of their minds. The Hunters had always revered the Elites as their commanders.

"There are only three because your fucking boss … your old boss, I mean … only had blood from three immortal dragons to power them. Of course, my kind are rare, which is another limiting factor, but immortal dragons are even rarer. I was made from a fourth immortal dragon's blood."

Blood which she hadn't been given in more than two months. Both she and her brother were dangerously low on power as a result, but they hadn't expected this trip to take so long. She could feel mortality creeping into her bones bit by bit, and just hoped they would last long enough to reach their dragons.

She pressed the bandage over his wound and gently sealed the tape at the edges.

"But Marcus …"

"He's alive and well. Mated to a dragon now." Abstractly, she realized Marcus was technically Zorion's stepfather, which made her mind twist into a knot. So was Nikhil, for that matter. And also the North brothers, who were Belah's other mates now. She wondered if the poor man realized he had so many father figures.

She tapped gently on the bandage. "All done now." She glanced up at him and took a step back from the heated look in his eyes. He moved to close the distance, his gaze flitting between her eyes and her mouth.

"Whoa, Paolo, don't you think you're taking forgiveness a step too far?" Neela asked, retreating farther.

The furtive sounds of skin on skin caught her attention, and she hazarded a glance toward the bunks. All the occupied beds now held naked men and they were *all* apparently enthralled enough by her presence to decide they needed to take care of business while she was in the room.

A chorus of rough pants and moans followed her backward retreat, her skin prickling from their gazes, and though she had no interest whatsoever in being their masturbatory inspiration, her nipples tightened and her core heated at the idea. God, that was all wrong, but as Paolo closed the distance and leaned down in an attempt to brush a kiss against her mouth, she caught the familiar scent of her brother's breath on his skin and understood.

"Fucking Naaz," she muttered, unable to avoid laughing. "Buddy, I'll take care of you," she said, grabbing the horny Hunter by the ears to hold him still. She leaned up so their mouths were aligned. Without actually touching her lips to his, she exhaled a bit of what scant power she had left. Blue smoke crept from her mouth to be inhaled by the Hunter. Within seconds, the lust in his gaze faded and he leaned back, blinking in surprise.

"Oh, shit … Please tell me I didn't touch you," he said, his eyes wide. "He set a trap for us, we knew that much, but we thought we were immune."

"Relax," she said. "Probably the pain of your wound caused a bit of a delay compared to your friends, though. They'll be at it for a few hours, but it'll wear off before they beat themselves bloody, don't worry." She grinned at his horrified reaction to the collection of masturbating men that surrounded them.

"Jesus. What the fuck, guys? There's a lady present!"

Contrary to his earlier behavior, he moved his body to block her view of the room and gripped her shoulders to turn her around. Clearly his intentions had changed, and all he wished was to protect her delicate sensibilities from the depraved behavior in the room.

She laughed as he followed her back into the corridor and yanked the curtain shut behind them, then visibly grimaced at the first drawn-out groan of one man orgasming, which was followed in quick succession by the others.

"Sorry," he said.

Neela shrugged. "I suppose we're even now. My poor, innocent soul will recover, I promise."

"I didn't think that. I know you're important to him. If he thinks we've damaged you …"

She rested a hand on his shoulder and squeezed. "I can take care of myself. If he doesn't get that, it isn't your fault. But I wouldn't mind some direction here. I need to find him, and he seems to have gone into hiding after our last conversation. Any idea where he is?"

Paolo shook his head. "He's not the most predictable boss. He always seems to show up when you're around, though, so my guess is he'll come to you eventually."

"Right. Eventually. I guess that's better than never, huh?" She gave him a small smile and left, uncertain what to do next.

She made it back to the bedroom she'd awakened in, but was too agitated to sleep. Besides, she didn't want to give him any excuses to visit her without the awareness of consciousness. Her bath had been cut short, so she decided to head back to the warm, fragrant pool he'd led her to earlier.

Once again, she stripped and stepped down into the luxurious heat. Candles still flickered around the entire room, flames he'd effortlessly extinguished and relit. She could control flames with her power, but not with quite as much ease. Still, she wanted to lure him back to her somehow, and if he was more comfortable in darkness, that's what she should give him.

She expelled a breath, her lungs burning from the use of the power twice in such a short time. It only reminded her that she *wasn't* a dragon, and that the magic that ran in her veins wasn't magic she'd been born with, even if she was capable of using it. With an effort of will, she pushed the magic through the room, methodically extinguishing the candles until only a single flame was still lit at the very edge of the bath.

The lone flickering fire and its reflection were barely enough for her to see beyond the water, and she decided to leave it lit. There had to be *some* compromise here. If she could convince him to come to her now, it would be a step forward.

"Zorion, please come back," she whispered, knowing he could hear her thoughts just fine if he wanted to. "I don't know why you're so afraid of showing yourself to me. What I saw was beautiful. I've waited almost my entire life for this. I was still young when Naaz and I found the first temple where you and your sister slept. I'd never had a lover before, and knew in that moment that you were meant to be my first."

She waded to the side of the pool where there was a submerged ledge and sat, waving her hands through the water as she kept speaking. Her throat constricted as she thought back to those early years when her faith in her commander had been destroyed, and she and her brother had begun to see Nikhil as a monster. It would be years before they understood that he'd been corrupted against his will, and what small amount of honor and love remained in him still struggled against the bonds of his captor.

How a man as strong as Nikhil could have been brought so low perplexed her, but she knew better than to disobey him after having once been so close to Zorion and having him taken away from her. She and Naaz had obediently followed after that. They had nothing else to live for, besides each other. Nikhil had nothing to live for then, period.

"You are still my first and only love, Z. You've been my soul's protector since the start. I am whole because you were there all along. And now I am offering myself to you, unconditionally, because I can't live without you anymore. So please, come to me. You can make it pitch black again, if you still fear me seeing too much, but I will love you no matter what. In the darkness or in broad daylight, I will never stop loving you."

A subtle draft sent a ripple across the water toward her. Neela's breath caught in anticipation of the dim light disappearing. The flame flickered and sputtered briefly, and she thought it would be fully extinguished, but the flame steadied and brightened.

She turned her head sharply as fabric rustled. The curtain that blocked the entrance to the room rippled and swayed as though a breeze had passed through it, but she could see no sign of a solid presence. Still, her skin prickled, and she knew she was being watched.

And then the candle light died.

Neela's pulse raced when a fresh draft blew past, teasing at the sensitive skin of her neck. The water in front of her surged as something big suddenly displaced it, pushing waves of heat up over the swell of her breasts.

Then he was there again, his solid shape only defined by the strange lights that ran beneath his skin. He was a contradiction of darkness and light. During that split-second when she'd seen his reflection earlier, his skin had seemed to absorb the light.

"Thank you," he said.

"Will you just tell me why?"

"Because I am different." He lifted one hand before his face, fingers splayed, then turned it. The lines of his palm glowed bright, the secrets of his destiny written there, if she only knew how to read it. But when he closed his fist, it seemed to disappear entirely. "I cannot assume a truly human appearance, no matter how hard I try. What you can see isn't what I wish to show you."

"I thought all dragons could transform themselves at will. Is it power you lack? Because maybe my Nirvana is enough …"

"I have power, Neela," he said. He took a step closer to her, pushing small waves up her chest again. She didn't move from her seat, but reflexively leaned back to adjust to his looming height when he stood before her looking down. He exhaled a glowing breath and hot, ethereal fingers began to tug at the end of her braid, slowly unraveling the tendrils of hair and fanning them around her shoulders. Then they brushed over her mouth, teasing the outline of her lips.

"Breathe me," he commanded.

Neela's sharp inhalation was a reflex to his touch more than anything. Her tongue tingled as the warmth passed her lips and flowed down her windpipe. Searing fire filled her lungs, making her gasp again. Gradually the heat flowed out into her body, the power that sank into her as vast and boundless as the universe. It shot through her bloodstream, filling her until her body felt like it contained the energy of an entire galaxy. She waved her fingers through the air and stars emerged, then planets, and within moments, entire solar systems floated around the room.

"How can you care about your looks when you have *this*?" she marveled.

"Because I want you. And you wish for a normal life. A lover, a family. A human life."

"I'm under no illusions about what my life is, Z. I want you no matter what. Being able to make love under the open sky, in a sundrenched field … where I can *smell* the sun … After an eternity living in a prison cell, is it any surprise that I want that? It doesn't matter to me how you look. Only that you're there. Unless … Can you not go out in daylight?"

"I can, but avoid it. I blend in better at night."

She chuckled. "I don't see how. You're all lit up." She slid off her seat and stood, placing a palm against his chest. He didn't move this time, but the fiery veins beneath his skin brightened.

"You light me up," he said. "I can control the fire inside me other times. Just not when you're near."

Neela licked her lips and darted a glance to his face. "You're saying I turn you on?" She slid her hands up his chest to rest at the tops of his shoulders, brushing her thumbs along the sides of his neck. With every stroke, little pulses of fire shot outward from the point of contact. Heat sank into her from his skin as though she was absorbing his power just through touch. She pulled closer until their legs touched under the water and his hard length brushed against her belly.

Warm arousal pooled between her thighs, amped up by the gentle caress of his fingers up her sides and back down until he rested his hands on her hips.

"What do you think?" he said, pulling her tighter against him.

She exhaled abruptly at the press of his massive shaft against her belly. All their endless nights talking in the dark of her cell, and never once had she ached so much to have him inside her. Being in that place had killed her desire to the point she'd been uncertain she would ever want sex. Being with Zorion in the flesh was a very different experience, however.

She hungered for him, and when she tugged his head down, the way he eagerly latched onto her mouth told her he was just as starved for this moment as she was. As his tongue swept into her mouth, followed by a groan of desire, she heard a mental plea echo through her mind.

"Please don't push me away again."

"Never. But we're revisiting the light thing later."

He dropped his hands to her backside and squeezed, pulling away from their kiss just enough to murmur, "As you wish." Then he hoisted her up his torso and she wrapped her legs around him, ready to let him take her however he wished.

The entire room brightened with surreal prismatic light, the fire in his skin reflecting off the water and bouncing off the walls in every direction. He cupped her breast like he had the first time, and she eagerly arched back, giving him access to bend his head and suck her nipple between his lips.

Everywhere they touched, his power seared her skin to the point she wouldn't have been surprised if she awakened the next day with welts all over her, but it wasn't pain so much as the white-hot pleasure of being touched by him after an eternity of craving this very thing.

She found herself laid flat on the warm stone at the edge of the pool, Zorion hungrily sucking at her breasts. He tilted his hips down and she moaned at the slow, deliberate way he grazed the entire length of his huge cock along the slick channel between her thighs.

He gripped her thighs, pushing them wide. His molten gaze swept down her body, heating her further.

"Put your hands above your head," he said, and she obeyed without a thought, her skin tingling in anticipation of more of those exquisite kisses and caresses that charged her entire body with immense magic.

"Why did you stop?" she whispered, confused by the way he'd paused, his cock on the verge of parting her and pushing inside. His chest heaved, and the brilliant fire that defined his cheekbones and his mouth made it evident that he was in the midst of some internal struggle.

"Forgive me for this, *adara*."

"For what?"

"I want to violate you the way I've watched so many others do. With you helpless and bound."

"But I'm neither," she said, yet when she tried to move her hands, she found them immobilized by glowing shackles. Her feet, too, were tethered to the edge of the pool by fetters made of fire, unable to move.

"If you don't want this, I will release you," he said, sliding his hands down the insides of her thighs until his thumbs grazed the outer folds of her pussy. The same perfect heat as before made her tilt her hips into his touch, and his cockhead pushed a little deeper. She couldn't move, which terrified her, but neither did she want him to stop.

"No. Let me see you first. I was blindfolded all those other times. I don't want to imagine the man who's fucking me. And I don't want to have this moment obscured from my memory by the lack of light. Show me your face, and you can have me any way you like."

"Neela …" he said, groaning in frustration.

Her core throbbed with the need to be stretched and filled by him, but the bindings were on the verge of throwing her into panic.

"Please. Lights. Then you'd better fuck me like you own my fucking soul, because you do."

Zorion's fingers dug into her thighs so hard she was sure she'd have bruises. The iridescent fire that threaded across his jaw flickered, telegraphing the clenching and unclenching of his teeth. Finally, he let out a deafening roar.

He slammed his cock into her, and the room went white.

CHAPTER 11

NEELA

$\mathcal{N}$eela screamed from the pleasure of that first piercing stroke, opening her up and filling her in a way she'd never been filled. When her mind cleared from the shock of it, she opened her eyes to the sight of vivid blue sky above.

Her gaze fell to the source of the pleasure: the thick length of cock ramming hard between her thighs and the glorious man attached to it.

But he wasn't a man. Despite the very tangible erotic sensations of their bodies connecting, now that she could see him in the daylight, she realized she could barely even see him at all. He was pure light. What was between the veins of fire before was nothing but translucent, shimmering space. The luminescent threads that defined his shape were still there, still blazing hotter with every stroke. But if she didn't know better, she'd have thought he was made of pure magic.

"I will have you. You promised." He pushed her legs wider, lifting her hips like she weighed nothing to spear her anew in a fresh, excruciatingly pleasurable angle. He pressed a thumb to her clit and tilted his head. "Will you come for me? Is this good?"

"Z … oh, god …" Neela's mind couldn't track the surreal turn this encounter had taken. The pleasure he drove through her made it even more difficult to process what was happening, but she nodded. "Yes. Make me come, please."

Bright power shot down his arm, through his thumb, and straight into her clit. The hot pulse of it acted instantaneously, throwing her into orbit with an agonized cry of pure ecstasy. She arched up, her head flying back while he continued to ram into her over and over, his strokes amplifying the pleasure of the orgasm that rocked her very being.

She had no time to process or even recover from the mind-shattering climax before he flipped her over and twisted his hand into her hair. She felt her head being pulled back by the length of thick black strands, his hand twining around and around ever tighter. Then he was inside her again from behind as she struggled to gain purchase on reality through the onslaught of his punishing thrusts.

Through it all, she had no time to be scared. He'd succeeded in shocking her so thoroughly with everything she needed, but hadn't known she craved. The pleasure she found in this rough treatment made no sense, but she loved it, loved the way he immobilized her with his hand in her hair and his cock inside her, impaling her with more vigorous thrusts.

She didn't know what the hell he was, whether he really even *was* a dragon, but whatever it was she loved it. Loved *him*.

"Take me, Z. Use me so hard you wipe out the memory of all those other goddamn cocks. Make me forget. Mark me from the inside out, baby."

His chest brushed against her back as he lowered himself over her, rutting against her like a wild beast now. Hot breath rushed past her ear, heavy panting making it clear how close to the edge he was.

"Your soul is mine, Neela. Your tight little cunt was never really fucked before, because *this* is what it means to be fucked. Those men were slaves, never worthy of your pleasure. Come for me again and show me how my cock owns you now."

His voice rumbled around her like thunder, despite the bright sun warming her back. The sounds vibrated through her body to her core, as though her very cells recognized the command he had over her pleasure, and they responded instantaneously, another surge of white-hot light blasting through her body.

As she cried out, his voice rose, his thrusts slowing but growing deeper, harder, and then stopping entirely. A deafening roar that shook the earth encompassed her and he released her hair, grabbing her hips with both hands as his cock surged and shot pulsing hot power deep into her.

Somehow she knew that what he was wasn't close to physical, and that the seed he'd just filled her womb with was pure magic as well. Her body felt lit up from the inside, and she abstractly wondered if the sun might get jealous by how brightly she must be shining at this very moment.

He started to pull out of her and she reached back, grabbing his hip and twisting around to look at him.

"Don't you dare run away from me now."

He exhaled a heavy breath. "I don't think I have the power to walk, much less carry us back to the warren."

"Good, because after that, I seriously need to be held. I think you touched my soul with your cock. It's a little tender."

He lowered himself over her again and wrapped his arms around her torso. As he pulled her to the ground against him, she took stock of where he'd taken her. Nothing but wild

Australian bush surrounded them. Somehow he'd managed to conjure a blanket for them to lay on, though, and for that, she was grateful.

Zorion's arm tightened around her, and he clutched her to his broad chest. If she closed her eyes, she could believe he was solid and made of warm flesh and bone, but the strange little pulses of fire that warmed the spots where they touched reminded her that something very different was at work here.

Taking a deep breath, she cautiously turned in his arms. She braced herself to face him in the daylight, and when her eyes met his, she caught a similar wariness in them.

Eyes … if they could even be called that. He was made of a web of filaments that merely bound tighter in the pair of lights where eyes should be. They were bright orbs with dots of fathomless black in the centers. Yet she could see the apprehension there regardless. Otherwise, his face was merely a suggestion of a face, like a watercolor artist had splashed colors onto a page, leaving a negative space in the shape of a man. It was the glow around him now that defined his shape more than the space he occupied.

"I get it now," she said. "Why the darkness makes more sense. You at least look close to solid in the shadows. What's the deal, Z? Why are you like this? Not that I'm complaining … Your parts all seem perfectly functional, but … I've never seen anything like you."

She lifted a hand to touch where his cheek should be. She met resistance that felt more like static than skin. A fringe of darker fire that almost resembled eyelashes obscured his gaze as he leaned into her touch.

The warm, pink fire of his lips tightened, and then he expelled a slow breath. "I am not yet whole, Neela. What I am to you now is merely the essence of my magic—my fire. More than just my breath sent out like a Shadow's to seduce and trick. This form is pure dragon fire. Every ounce of power that sustains me made into something as close to human as I can shape it."

She frowned, drifting her hand down over his shoulder and chest, marveling at how very solid he still felt despite the crackle of energy that tickled her palm. "Where is the rest of you, if you aren't whole?"

"In the temple, still in stasis. When I figured out how to send my power out along with my fire, I knew I had to meet you this way first. I don't want you to wake my body. Stay with me like this, if you can find it in yourself to accept this part of me."

"But I want *all* of you, Z. Don't you want to be whole?"

"The creature that sleeps in the temple is a monster. Trust me, it isn't something you want to see."

"You were afraid to show yourself to me like this. I survived it. I think I can survive seeing your physical body too. I want *all* of you. I'm committed to the whole package, good or bad. You got all of me, including a very disturbing kink I didn't even know I had."

"It isn't my appearance that I wish to protect you from. I am pure light in this form. My dragon fire is the magic that defines this body, but half of my power was darkness, too. You know who my father is. The combination of his and my mother's power within me magnified that darkness. Then I watched while you were hurt, and took that pain away from you. The darkness I protected you from is inside that part of me."

"Oh, god, no wonder you left it behind." She pressed her lips together. "I think it's time for me to face it. You shouldn't have to bear that burden for me, not if it means you sacrificing your true form."

"What kind of protector would I be if I forced you to take back the pain I shielded you from? I won't do that. We can stay here, like this. I have more than enough power to make you happy."

She sighed and shook her head. "It isn't just about us, though. Asha's father needs us back. All of us. You should know that." Her voice grew strident as emotion gripped her chest.

"You know what's at stake," she said more softly. He'd been inside her mind the night when Nikhil had come to her, and then again only a few weeks later when the tiny life inside her body was stolen away. He'd comforted her as well as he could through that loss that had left her more raw than any of the other violations of her body.

Zorion remained still, his gaze turned away from her and the fire flowing through his veins pulsing with a rhythm that matched her heartbeat. Racing with uncertainty.

She reached up and squeezed his shoulder. "Come with me like this, then. You can travel as easily as a drift. Quicker even than Naaz or I could, once we're outside the zone of the temple. We can work out how to deal with your body later, but we need you and Asha to fight this battle.

"I don't even know what's happening with the army now. For all I know, they're already confronting the Ultiori mercenaries in Egypt, but we need to leave within the next day. Nikhil wants us back by the Equinox, because that's when he expects Meri to make her move."

"Neela … I can't. This is my essence, not all of me. I'm still tethered to my physical body. I am not capable of traveling beyond the range of that tether."

"What do you think will happen if I awaken your body?"

"What I did to you … possessing you like a wild fiend … the creature that sleeps in the temple craves that and more. Pain and humiliation and defilement. That part of me desires those things so much I couldn't even shake all of it. I craved it like a drunk craves spirit, but the taste you gave me was enough for this part of me to be satisfied. It won't be enough for him. He would destroy you, and revel in your annihilation. I can't let that happen to you."

"But I helped make him that way … it isn't fair," she said in a small voice, tears burning her eyelids.

"Asha will be free to go. You can leave me, if you wish, but I can't leave this place if I want to protect you. Please don't ask that of me, *adara*."

"All right," she said, sinking into his arms, her heart aching at the thought of what darkness he had borne for her sake that had corrupted his soul to such a degree he had to protect her from it. She took a deep breath and tilted her head up, pressing her lips to the bow-shaped fire above his chin.

At least she had this, and it was infinitely more than she'd ever hoped for.

As he pushed her back to the ground and proceeded to make love to her again, she surrendered to his power completely, her body reacting with fresh heat to the more tender touch he gave her this time. Even without the bindings he'd controlled her with before, he drew her climax from her again and again, proving repeatedly that he owned her soul.

But as he filled her with the bright power of his magic again, that darkness beckoned, its pull every bit as inevitable as the beacon of light that had drawn her to this part of him to begin with.

CHAPTER 12

NEELA

$\mathcal{N}$eela lay awake in the darkness of a huge bedchamber, her back tingling with the warmth of Zorion's magic curling around her. He slept soundly, the light of his fire all but extinguished in his slumber. After eons of spending her nights in a pitch black cell, it was a comfort to have this glow surrounding her now.

The wild bush he'd transported them to earlier had been an idyllic spot for a lovers' first tryst, with the sunlit sky above and wild Outback flowers blooming around them while they made love. Each time he'd been gentler with his touch, seeming to find less and less pleasure in the act of immobilizing her and taking her rough.

Yet her craving for that kind of dominance grew, until she had to restrain herself from begging him to hurt her. She couldn't bear to ask for it, not after she'd seen his distaste over voicing his need to bind her. At the end of their love-making, she'd only found pleasure when she'd been on her knees with his cock filling her mouth and a conjured version of it impaling her core. She could almost imagine the dark version of him taking her while the light one was pleasured by her mouth. And when he'd shot his liquid fire down her throat, she had come harder than any other time before.

She still had the hot taste of him on her tongue, but forced herself to banish the wish that he'd wake and tie her to the bed and ride her hard like he had the first time. She extracted herself from his embrace and eased off the mattress, then padded to the separate chamber where the privy was. When she returned, she stood at the end of the bed, watching him and unable to shake the feeling that something crucial was missing.

It could just be the mark itself. He'd confessed that he couldn't mark her without the proper implement. A dragon marked with its true tongue. Even though Zorion had command of most of his magic, without being able to manifest that part, he could never truly mark her, either. She'd been disappointed by that news, though he'd distracted her easily by proving how talented his magic tongue could be. But she hadn't forgotten.

In the back of her mind, that darkness still beckoned, and now she knew what it was. The other half of him waited for her, and she was due to take her burden back.

She silently retrieved her clothes and slipped away, dressing in the darkened corridor outside the chamber they'd shared. Then she made her way to the barracks and shook a sleeping Paolo by the shoulder.

He blinked and grumbled, but his eyes brightened when he saw her.

"Hey. What's up?"

"I need to know how the hell to get out of this place."

"Boss man didn't show you?"

"No. He's asleep, and I don't want to wake him."

Paolo gave her an uncertain look. "If he didn't give you access, I don't know if I should."

"I need to get to the temple," she said. "Naaz needs me."

She tacked the last part on as an afterthought. She had no idea how much these guys knew about what she and her brother were after. The majority of Ultiori Hunters were kept in the dark about the finer points of dragon hibernations. They only needed to know how to hunt the ones who were awake, after all, and couldn't have accessed any of the hibernation temples if they'd wanted to. That was a detail the Ultiori had learned early on. Dragons didn't fuck around when it came to protecting their offspring.

Paolo rubbed a hand over his face and swung his legs over the edge of the bed. "Need me to wake the others? Surely the boss would want to know if your brother's in trouble. We probably owe you guys, after the shit we put you through for the last two months."

"No!" she blurted, then took a deep breath. "I mean, Zorion's wiped out. It isn't dire. I just need to get to the temple … It's kind of a family thing. Personal."

He was still clad in pants and slipped his feet into the boots left on the floor beside his bunk. Rising, he grabbed a shirt and nodded at her as he pulled it on.

"C'mon, it's this way."

Exhaling with relief, she followed him out the door. They wound around the corridor and into the break room. Three of the other Hunters glanced up from their card game. Paolo cursed and stalked over to the table. He picked up the empty bottle that sat at the edge and waved it in the air.

"What gives, guys? This was supposed to last us two more days."

"Don't worry man. Phillips went to restock."

"Does the boss know? You know we've gotta get approval for shit like this."

"Boss was indisposed," one of the men said, giving Neela a sidelong look.

"Fuck. Well, it's not on me if he loses his shit. Make sure

he knows that."

He started to walk away and Neela fell into step. As they reached the exit to the room, he paused and turned back. "You guys didn't see us, got it?"

The trio of Hunters chuckled. One guy nodded. "Fair enough. Nobody broke any rules tonight. Not one." Neela caught a wink as Paolo gripped her arm and urged her on.

She thought she'd explored the place thoroughly the day before, but when the floor started to gradually incline, she knew they were in a section she hadn't seen.

"How the hell did I miss this?"

"You gotta know it's there. The opening's not visible except from the right angle, and the place is arranged so you tend to always travel the corridors in one direction. You'd have found it eventually."

Within moments, they emerged through a rock face onto a ledge overlooking a canyon. It was the same narrow canyon she and Naaz had last been ambushed in on their way to the temple.

"Path down is there," Paulo said, pointing to a shadowy area behind a scrubby bush.

"Thank you. I owe you one," she said, giving his arm a squeeze.

His brows furrowed as he nodded. "You sure you're cool? I can come with. Make sure the dingoes don't get you."

Neela chuckled and patted the blade at her belt. "As long as I don't get ambushed by Hunters again, I'll be fine. I'm wise to you guys now ... and I've kind of got the goods on your boss."

He nodded and smiled. "I sure wouldn't want to meet either you or your brother alone. We weren't aiming to kill you, but the way you laid us out both times, I don't think you were in any danger. We're fucking lucky we work for *him* now. Doctor Waters would've left us to rot."

"The doctor ruined everyone's lives," Neela said. "It's time for retribution. Stick with him and you guys will do fine, deal?"

Paolo laughed. "Nobody pays better than him. I doubt any of the guys are in a hurry to cut and run."

He remained on the ledge, his gaze following her as she descended the treacherous path to the canyon floor. When she reached the bottom, she paused and closed her eyes, reaching out for that shadow of an impression she'd sensed before, but hadn't understood. Zorion's magic still floated like a bright light at the back of her mind, but she knew now that wasn't all of him.

She didn't know what she would find when she awakened his true body, but whatever darkness corrupted him now was hers to bear. She'd been strong enough to survive without him for so long. She had to give him a chance to be whole, and the cravings he'd awakened in her the past day made her certain she could handle whatever darkness the other half of him was made of.

The dark presence pulsed at the core of her mind, each beat reflected in a similar throb between her thighs. Zorion's lighter half had satisfied her well, but she was still left wanting. It made no sense to her that she should harbor such dark cravings, after all she'd lived through.

She couldn't bear the thought of part of him left to the darkness, forced to remain trapped in a stone prison the way she'd been trapped for most of her life.

She reached the canyon floor and the spot where she and Naaz had parted ways. He'd been right all along, his tracks moving off in the direction the shadowy pulses drew her. He was in the arms of Asha now, his damaged soul made whole by the light within his dragon. It was Neela's duty to do the same for Zorion.

"Where do you think you're going, little breeder?"

She jumped at the grating voice that came from the shadows to one side of the path. She'd been so focused on reaching the temple she hadn't been alert to her surroundings. A chill went down her spite at the sound of that voice. Squinting into the darkness, she saw a vaguely human shape squatting atop a big boulder.

It was a Hunter, judging by the details of his clothing she could make out in the shadows. He wore black fatigues with a knife at his belt and held a length of rope in one hand. He was toying with the rope, coiling it into loops and uncoiling it again.

"Are you Phillips? Your buddies are waiting for the whiskey, you know. You don't need to follow me—I'm fine without a bodyguard."

"You've strayed just a little too far from your master, Elite. Time for me to bring you home. That warm little oven of yours is too valuable to let some filthy dragon fill it up."

That voice again ... the strange pitch made no sense coming from a burly man like the Hunter who watched her. It sounded like the voice of a woman who'd survived being strangled, and made Neela's mind itch like insects were crawling inside her skull.

Her skin prickled. The day Nikhil had arrived in her cell and they'd made love, silently agreeing to the union out of self-preservation more than desire. Shortly afterward, their true master had appeared. Nikhil's behavior had shifted instantly, his eyes going blank and soulless when the woman in the lab coat smiled. He'd left without so much as a backward glance after a night of pure tenderness.

The contrast was jarring, but more alarming was the feeling Neela had had afterward. Like some foul creature had defiled the inside of her head. Despite the fact that she'd viewed Nikhil as a father her entire life, making love to him hadn't felt dirty. But in the moments after Meri had visited that day, she couldn't scrub her skin hard enough to feel clean.

She felt the same way now.

"Meri. It's too fucking late. I'll never let you touch me again. If you let that man near me, I'll slit his fucking throat. There's nothing you can do."

"He doesn't need to get near you, breeder. He's skilled enough to do just what I need from here."

"What, come and talk shit to me? I've had about three thousand years too much of your shit. Get the fuck over yourself."

The man shook his head and made a tutting sound with his tongue. "You've grown bold in your freedom, slave. You and your brother were nothing more than the worthless spawn of a dragon's whores. You have one thing that makes you special, and I'm here to take that back. And once I have you, I'll take your brother back too. It's time you returned to serve me before I take control of my home."

The man's eyes swirled with a disorienting whirlpool of light. Before Neela could react, his hand whipped out, the coil of dark leather unfurling in the darkness, barely visible as it sailed toward her. The cracking sound betrayed the nature of what he'd held. Not a rope, but a whip, and the lash had just snapped tight around her throat.

She tried to cry out, but her throat constricted, her breath cut short by the sudden yank of a strong arm on the other end. Scrabbling and clawing at it did no good. She stumbled, eyes wide and tears falling as the man with the wild nymph's eyes hauled her toward the boulder he sat on, pulling hand over hand on the whip until she was dangling against the side, kicking at air and grasping at her throat.

"*Zorion! Need you!*" The desperate cry shot from her mind just as her vision went black.

CHAPTER 13

NAAZ

*N*aaz jolted awake and scrambled up out of bed, driven to action by the horrifying dream he'd just had. His sister was in danger. *Real* danger.

"What is wrong?" Asha asked, staring wide-eyed at him from a nest of silken sheets.

"It's Neela. Something's happened. I mean … something happened before I got here, but this is worse."

"Can I help?"

He paused with his boots half-laced and looked at her. "Yeah, about that … I kind of came here for your help to begin with. I shouldn't have gotten distracted for so long. I need you to help me find her."

"I know." She gave him the sweetest smile, her lovely skin shimmering with subtle inner fire. "You were afraid to hurt my feelings before. Tell me what happened to her."

He gave her the short version of the repeated attacks they'd endured that made their travels such an ordeal, all of them culminating in the one that had separated him and his sister.

"Something feels different about this, though. I've always had a sense of when she's in danger. When she was taken by that man, I was *worried* … he made threats. But I never felt like *this*. We still had a link that made me sure she was out there and unharmed, until now …"

"Now you're not so sure she's alive?"

"Yeah … and that scares the shit out of me."

"What did he look like? The man who took her."

He opened his mouth to describe Neela's kidnapper, then closed it again, uncertain how to explain his odd appearance. "It was like he was made of night, darkness, with this crazy fire under his skin. Kind of the exact opposite of you, in fact."

He stared at her bare breasts where the web of tiny veins was most concentrated, growing denser toward her nipples, which seemed to brighten under his gaze. They hardened, and she lifted her hands to cover them.

"Is there something wrong with my breasts?"

"No … it's just … He was like you. Oh, god." Naaz's brain churned as he put the pieces together. The way she'd argued about the direction of the temple, and then the creature who had taken her, so similar to Asha, yet so very different. "Zorion did this."

Rage warred with panic inside him and he threw on the rest of his clothes. "If that fucker's hurt her, I will kill him. I don't care how long it's been since I've shed dragon blood, I will fucking end his life."

He finally paused long enough to see the stricken look on Asha's face and gritted his teeth.

"Zorion wouldn't. He loves her," she said. "And I know him. He's protective. He'd never hurt her. He'd be more likely to hurt *you* for touching me, but it's too late for him to worry about that, because you're mine now."

As if in response to her declaration, his entire back

tingled with the fresh mark she'd given him partway through their lovemaking.

"All I know is that something bad has happened, and he was the last person who had her. If it's him, and she's hurt … I won't make any promises, baby."

She pressed her lips into a hard line and nodded. "I know where to start."

She hopped off the bed and strode toward the door. As she walked, a cloud of shimmering smoke flowed from her mouth and nose, weaving itself into an outfit not unlike the one he wore. The cargo pants and boots fit her well, but looked extremely out of place against her fair, luminescent skin. But a second later that changed too, until she was simply a lovely human woman dressed for battle.

He followed her out into the corridor beyond the big door to her chamber, but she didn't go far. She strode several paces then stopped outside the other set of big double doors in that hallway. The monolithic carved black opal loomed in front of Naaz.

Asha leaned her ear close and knocked daintily on the surface.

"Zorion, are you awake? Naaz needs to ask you some questions."

Naaz tilted his head. "Ah … he didn't bring her back here, did he? We'd have known."

"She isn't here, but he is. And if he took her, he'd know."

"But he can't be here … not if he's out there."

"He's been here since they moved us in. I would know if he'd left."

She leaned against the doors and they slowly swung inward, revealing a maw of pure midnight so impenetrable it was disconcerting to look at. *Nothingness* was what came to mind, and Naaz nearly yelled out an objection when Asha took a step across the threshold, fearing she'd fall into an abyss.

But the veil of night parted for her, the luminosity of her skin piercing it and her brilliance flooding the room. When she was several yards in, she turned.

"Are you coming? He's in here."

Naaz hesitated before moving toward her, his skin prickling with dread despite his conviction that he'd seen Zorion *outside* the temple. He recalled what the man had said now ... the threats he'd made, forcing Naaz to choose between Asha or his sister. But if that had been Zorion, what the hell was still inside the temple where Zorion should have been?

Asha reached out a hand and he took it, letting her lead him farther into the murky darkness.

"Doesn't this seem ... off to you?" he whispered.

"He's been like this since we moved in. *Broody.*"

"Jesus. If this is broody, I'd hate to see him in a really bad mood."

"You have to understand, we've waited a long time for you and your sister. He's probably just a little envious that you came first. But if his fire has your sister, he will want to know."

"His ... fire?"

"I think that's what you saw out there. My brother's fire left him a couple months ago ... not long after we were sealed in. Without it, we get this." She let out a weary sigh and waved around at the darkness.

"Is ... one side good and one evil?" Naaz asked, bombarded with paranoid images of some kind of Jekyll and Hyde creature who was destined to mate with his sister. He needed to figure this out, and fast, but for now, he was back to the conviction that he might have to get on board with killing a dragon again.

Asha laughed and rolled her eyes. "He's just Zorion. My big brother. You'll get used to him."

A vague shape coalesced out of the shadows, and Naaz squinted to try to make sense of it. A few steps farther in, he recognized a sarcophagus similar to the one Asha had slept in. This one was clearly male, with a rigid outline of a phallus cast in stone in an exaggerated size and shape. It was so far from representing a human male, Naaz nearly laughed at the absurdity of it.

It mattered little now. "Can you talk to him?" he asked.

"We both can after we wake him up. Now that we're both awake, it should be easy."

"No fucking way," Naaz said, stepping in front of her and pushing her backward. "That's Neela's job, not yours. I mean, he's your *brother*, for fuck's sake!"

"Not like that! Ugh, no." She gripped his hands and squeezed, bringing them up to cover her breasts. Her nipples were hard beneath the fabric of her conjured shirt. "You and me together, just close enough for him to have *your* Nirvana. I'll hold back. Neela's your blood, so it should work."

Naaz's cock hardened at the mere suggestion of bedding her again, and when she arched her chest into his palms, he couldn't help but squeeze both luscious orbs. The fabric of her shirt dissolved, leaving him in contact with Asha's bare skin and hard nipples.

You've done far worse than make love to a girl in front of her brother, he told himself. And this particular girl was one he'd happily make love to anytime and anyplace she asked for it.

She turned, a slow smile spreading across her face as she backed up toward the sarcophagus. Its dark, polished stone reflected the glowing fire beneath her skin as her bare backside came to rest against it.

"God, you drive me wild," Naaz murmured against her ear, burying his face against her neck and kissing his way down her shoulder. "This had better work, and he'd better fucking have some answers if it does."

"He will," she said as she pushed Naaz's shirt up, tracing tiny circles around his nipples before tearing at his belt buckle and the closure of his pants.

He bent and closed his lips around one delicious ripe cherry of a nipple, groaning against her skin as she lifted her legs to wrap them around his hips. With one hand, she stroked his cock and aimed it at her entrance. Then he was lost to her, staring down into the iridescent fire of her eyes and burying himself into her to the hilt.

Asha's head flew back and she exhaled a half-moan, half-sigh when he began to fuck her, slowly at first, then harder and with more urgency. She clung to him, lifting her hips to meet his, and gripped at the back of his neck, forcing his head down to meet her lips.

Naaz braced both hands on the warm opal of the sarcophagus, barely conscious of the growing heat beneath his palms. He was too lost in her to care when a fissure appeared beneath his fingers just as his orgasm took hold.

The cover split in two when he yelled Asha's name, his semen shooting deep into her tight channel. Her nails raked delicious furrows of fire down his back, his entire body lighting up with pleasure.

"Don't stop!" she cried.

His cock wasn't close to soft, so he kept fucking, the orgasm fading, but another building swiftly. It was as though he'd become a conduit for pleasure, and it was flowing straight through his body. But unlike the first few times he'd made love to her, the power wasn't going to her. It went into the stone behind her.

He was too consumed by ecstasy to make sense of what happened next. Her soft heat was all that mattered, so when the opposite side of the sarcophagus flew back and smashed into pieces and a dark shape emerged, he couldn't stop.

The last thing he remembered before Asha's cry of pleasure was the gargantuan shape of a dragon launching into the air and smashing through the ceiling above. A roar sounded, echoing over the din of stones crashing down around them. In that roar, Naaz was nearly certain he'd heard his sister's name.

Zorion woke to the panicked cry of his lover, every thread of magic that defined his shape lighting up like the sun. She wasn't in the bed next to him. Focusing on the origin of that call, he went, the magic transporting him instantly to the location where the cry had originated.

The imprint of her fear was burned into the air, but Neela was nowhere to be found. Only the kicked up dust before a large boulder betrayed that someone had been here. Someone who had struggled.

He couldn't sense her, either, no matter how far he reached, and the inability to find even a faint sign of her presence made him panic. He transported himself to the very edge of his new prison—a prison he'd forced himself to accept—yet found no hint that she was anywhere within these boundaries. But even if she had gone outside them, he'd have sensed her. Their minds had been linked for millennia —ever since she'd first found him and touched the black stone sarcophagus of his prison. He'd been able to communicate with her mind, her very soul, all that time.

He never knew how much he'd come to love that sense of her until now.

"Neela!" he bellowed from the top of the boulder where she'd last been.

A thunderous roar answered, and his eyes shot to the sky. "Sweet Mother, no! Not you!"

A dark shape circled above, wingtips shining with what remnants of inner fire still remained after Zorion had left his physical form. How had his body awakened without her? For a split-second, he had a spark of hope. Had she gone to the temple? Had his shadow hidden her from him?

The creature spiraled around the canyon, black smoke billowing from its maw. It had no fire, but it had power. If he had to fight to get her back, it wouldn't be pretty.

"What have you done with her?!" he yelled at his shadow when it lowered itself to the canyon floor, wings flapping to steady its descent.

The creature landed, churning up dust and rocks and crushing several bushes beneath its huge bulk. Then it shifted, shrinking into the shape of a flesh and blood man with skin the color of night. The sight was a harsh reminder of what Zorion lacked, being made of pure dragon fire with no physical aspect of his own. He could mimic that shape, but could never truly have a body.

The ebony-skinned man tilted his head, studying Zorion for several moments before he spoke, his voice hard. "You betray her pain by denying me. We cannot exist without her —she cannot fully love without us both."

"I'm protecting her from what you've become. She deserves a life free of those things that were done to her. If you love her, you'll keep those memories far away."

"None of us can be free if we don't acknowledge the walls we build around our own souls. *I* can free her by showing her the way to break them down. All you wish to do is hide the darkness from her, but it will always be there. I will *always* be there. You know this as much as I do."

"You shouldn't even be free! If she didn't wake you, how did you get out?"

A resonant roar echoed through the canyon, and Zorion jerked his gaze skyward. A shimmering white shape soared overhead, a darker figure riding astride. Asha banked and twisted, toying with the warm currents before descending. Zorion was too overcome by worry to be happy for his sister, but he had his answer. Somehow Asha and her new mate had figured out how to wake up his darker half.

"Where is she?!" he yelled.

"Taken while you slept," his shadow answered. "You could never be enough for her. After all the time we spent sharing her mind, her soul, surely you realized we couldn't take all her darkness. She needs us both."

Asha landed, and her lover slid from her back and jogged toward them. Naaz's blue gaze was startlingly similar to his sister's, and a fresh pang of worry shot through Zorion. The involuntary reaction was telegraphed into the darkness with a surge of light from the center of his chest.

Naaz blinked at him, frowned, and turned to the more solid figure that stood facing him.

"Which one of you is the true Zorion?"

"I am," they both said in unison.

Naaz uttered a soft curse. "One of you had better tell me what the fuck happened to my sister."

"Taken," Zorion's dark half said. "I know not where, nor if she is even alive."

"They can't have gone far. The temple's wards prevent drifting within a hundred miles. If it's the Ultiori, they'd have to carry her over land," Naaz said.

His gaze shot to the canyon's edge, and he drew his blade.

Zorion followed the direction of his gaze to the canyon face high above where the entrance to the warrens were concealed. Several figures were making their way down the rocky path.

"We heard your rally call, boss," Paolo said when he reached them.

"Where's the last?" Zorion asked.

"Phillips never returned from his whiskey run last night."

"Did you lose one of your pets?" his dark half asked, taunting him.

"Where?" Zorion snapped, cursing himself for losing track. He'd had such a tight leash on all the men ever since discovering their little Ultiori cell and taking the time to break the spell Meri had over their minds. They'd been loyal to him for months without much effort beyond keeping mental tabs on them. Human men were easily influenced with either money, drink, or women, and two out of three generally did the trick. But he couldn't influence them beyond the range of his power, which was limited by the location of the infernal dark creature who stood glaring at him now.

"Warburton, boss."

"That's where Neela and I flew in two months ago," Naaz said. "It's miles outside the zone." He clenched his jaw as he shot a fierce glance between Zorion and the men who had joined them. "Are these fuckers following *you*? Have they been all this time?"

"Since Midwinter," Zorion said. The Solstice was the first moment he'd been able to gather the power to push his fire beyond the confines of his prison. "I found their camp not far from the temple. It seems Meri keeps tabs on all the dragon temples, but has pulled her men from all but this one. It was easy for me to break her hold on their minds, once I learned the trick to controlling them."

"We ran out of whiskey," Paolo offered with a shrug.

"And the only female within a hundred miles was locked inside that temple," one of the other men said.

"Are you sure you guys were Hunters?" Naaz asked, gaping at the group.

"Their darkest cravings were enhanced when I discovered them. Once I cleansed their minds of Meri's influence, they became more human again. Meri's power corrupts. Without that influence, they are honorable, loyal men. Provided I remember to pay them. It seems I must have lost track of that detail when you and your sister arrived."

"If you've been their boss for the last three months … that means you're the bastard who slowed us down." He shot a look to Zorion's dark half, who simply shook his head and pointed, shedding all blame.

"My sister's important to me," Zorion said. "I couldn't very well let a man near her who hadn't earned the right. You proved yourself adequately."

"Proved myself?" Naaz said. "What the actual fuck, man? Do you know what I had to go through for the past *three thousand* years?"

"Did you feel worthy of Asha two days ago?" Zorion asked. "Until I gave you something else to fight for, you were floundering. You didn't believe waking her was a high enough purpose. You needed a selfless goal to justify taking that step. Making you think Neela was in danger worked, but your sister was safe."

Naaz's eyes flashed with rage and he bared his teeth. "If she's so safe, where the fuck is she now? You lost my sister, didn't you? Somehow you lost control of your fucking dogs, and she's paying for it. It's a two-hour drive to Warburton on those shitty little roads we walked to get here. If the asshole who took her has a Jeep, he could have her on a goddamn plane by now. I don't know what your plan is, but I'm going to save her before Meri gets her hands on my sister again. You have no fucking idea what she went through while stuck in that prison."

"I know *everything* she went through," Zorion's dark half said. "I'll follow. Lead the way, brother."

Naaz climbed onto Asha's back again, and the trio was airborne before Zorion could object.

"What's the plan, boss?" Paolo asked. "We going after her?"

Zorion followed the dark shape of his physical body until he could no longer see it against the night sky. The tether tugged, but he waited just a little longer. The darkness that drove that creature was something he'd just as soon have left locked inside the temple forever, but now that it was out, he had no choice but to follow.

"To me," Zorion commanded. The men obeyed, circling around him and resting hands on whatever parts of his outstretched arms they could reach. When they were all in contact, he closed his eyes and reached for the new boundary of his power, which shifted with every flap of his dark half's wings. When he sensed the town Paolo had mentioned come into range, he moved, teleporting his entire squadron to the outskirts.

The drone of an airplane engine drowned out any other sound. He still couldn't find a glimmer of Neela's mind, no matter how hard he tried.

"Find Phillips," he commanded. "I'll start looking for Neela."

Paolo hesitated. "The doctor ..." he said with a worried frown.

"You stay within range of my power, you're fine. Phillips strayed outside that zone."

"We're with you, boss, as long as you want us. What should we do when we find Phillips?"

Zorion resisted giving a kill order, though it was tempting. The man wasn't in control of his actions. They'd all been Meri's puppets, and didn't deserve to die for it. Phillips' only weakness was his need for booze, and chances were he'd found a woman while he was out too. If Zorion hoped to keep the men loyal, he'd have to remedy the third item to make sure they didn't stray again.

But now that his dark half was free, their entire future was uncertain. He might be forced to tag along wherever the dragon went, but he'd be damned if he merged with it again. He'd die before he inflicted that darkness on Neela.

The men scattered. Some drifted, their bodies fading like smoke, while others jogged away to closer targets.

A chorus of flapping wings approached, and he braced himself for more recriminations from Neela's brother and his own dark half. They were justified, though. He should have sensed Neela's departure, kept an eye on her, but they'd fallen asleep, tangled in each other's arms after making love all afternoon. She hadn't run after he'd fulfilled that singular craving he'd had for so long. That was a good sign that she was willing to stay, or at least not seek out more than he was willing to offer.

He watched them approach, his sister looking like she belonged beside Naaz, wearing the same black fatigues with her pale hair woven in a braid at the back of her neck. The darker forms of Neela's brother and Zorion's more sinister reflection flanked her.

Naaz opened his mouth to speak, but stopped short, his eyes widening at something past Zorion's shoulder. Zorion turned to see a small plane starting to taxi with three of his mercenaries running toward it.

Paolo materialized beside him, breathless.

"She's inside, boss. Phillips is dead. There are half a dozen other Hunters in the plane, all armed to the teeth. We've gotta take them down before they get airborne."

He had a stricken look that set off alarm bells in Zorion's head. "What aren't you telling me?"

Paulo shook his head. "She didn't look good … They had her hooked up to machines like Doctor Waters used in her lab. Her head was shaved with …" He wiggled his fingers over his skull. "With things stuck to it. Monitors showed a heartbeat, but someone said something about no brain activity."

"I don't know what the fuck that means," Zorion growled.

"Fuck no. Don't you fucking tell me that!" Naaz yelled. Turning, he pointed a finger into Zorion's face. "If you don't come with me, I'm going in alone. Asha, stay here, baby. This is going to get ugly."

With that, Naaz disappeared, leaving behind only a wisp of red smoke.

"I think it means she's brain dead, boss," Paolo said softly. "Her heart beats, but her mind is gone."

Denial shackled Zorion to the ground. An angry yell pierced the air. The sound hadn't come from him, though the howl inside his own mind was a perfect reflection of the anger in his darker half's explosive cry. Zorion reacted instantly to that sound, his fire blazing hot, propelling him as quickly as sunlight toward the plane that still taxied, picking up speed as it made its way toward the runway.

"No!" The yell was a command that yanked him back. "You were the cause of this," his ebony reflection snarled. "Too fucking afraid of how perfect I might be for her. She needs *me* more than she needs you. She was coming for me when she was taken. I could feel her close. I heard her call before you even woke up."

"Then let's fucking make it right!" he yelled back. "Get over there and stop that fucking thing!"

The darkness grew around them, inky black blotting out everything but his sister's anxious glow and his own fire. "What do you think I'm doing?" his dark half spat.

The agony of realization hit, Zorion's heart shattering at what he'd caused, what he knew to be true. *I want all of you,* she had said, and he knew she'd meant it. He'd protected her for so long from darkness, but he couldn't block all of it. Not even the worst of it, he realized. He never had any hope of saving her from the one thing that might have destroyed a woman weaker than Neela, yet here she was, seeking him out despite that loss.

"You finally getting it?" his darker half asked. "Come back to me and we can make this right."

The plane was moving faster now, too fast for the mercenaries to keep up with on foot. Several drifted out of sight, and he caught movement within the small windows of the plane. The door flew open and a man sailed out, hitting the pavement in a crumpled heap. Not one of his men, he was gratified to see.

"Zorion, what are you waiting for?" his sister yelled.

"Go!" he commanded the dark figure who stood waiting before him. "I'm with you."

His ebony reflection transformed into his true shape and took to the air, soaring above until he came down again in the center of the runway in front of the plane. More pitch black smoke billowed out of his mouth, immersing them in pure darkness that only his and Asha's fire could penetrate.

"Come, sister," he said, reaching out a hand.

They appeared inside the cabin amid a bloody massacre. Naaz had his blade out, blood streaking his face, tangled in a brutal fight with a Hunter. Two of Zorion's own mercenaries were in similar straits.

Zorion ignored the others, heading straight to the gurney strapped down in the rear of the plane with Neela's unconscious body strapped to it. Wires and tubes ran everywhere, connected to beeping monitors with blips of iridescent light glowing through the darkness.

The plane lurched to a sudden stop amid the sound of smashing glass. Then metal twisted and groaned, the entire cabin lurching from side to side. Asha let out a cry and grabbed at one of the seatbacks for balance. She took a deep breath and expelled a puff of bright white smoke that swirled around Naaz, creating a forcefield about an inch away from his skin. She did the same for Neela.

"I can't tell them apart!" she yelled, giving Zorion an anxious look. "Which ones work for you?"

Zorion was busy unstrapping Neela's body and yanking the electrodes off her bare scalp. His heart ached at the naked vulnerability of her now. They'd taken everything—her clothes, her hair, her mind. She had nothing, not even a spark left for him to cleanse of darkness with his fire. When he pulled the tube from her throat, she expelled one breath, but her lungs failed to inflate again.

Around him, eerie laughter filled the cabin. Naaz stumbled back in shock from the man whose chest he'd just buried his blade in. The other enemies all cackled in perfect synchronicity, and then their voices joined in harmony.

"I will find another, if I can't have her. There are bound to be other Blessed females out there whose wombs are ripe for my use. I'll let you have hers back, since she's useless to you now. Her mind wasn't necessary for me to fill her with another baby to suit my needs. I'll be in the Haven soon enough. When I get to the Source, you are all doomed."

Rending steel drowned out the rest of their enemy's speech, and Zorion's dark half tore the side of the plane apart. His black-scaled snout plunged in, followed by a big taloned claw. He grabbed two of the enemy soldiers, tearing them to pieces before reaching for a third. It gave

Zorion's men the distraction they needed to finish off the last three.

The destroyed plane lurched to the side. Acrid smoke filled the cabin, the men coughing and trying to catch their breath as they drifted out one by one to get away from the impending fire.

"Get Neela!" Naaz yelled at Zorion as he grabbed Asha around the waist, and the pair disappeared in a cloud of red. Zorion's monstrous shadow reached a talon in, snapping the remaining straps that held Neela to the gurney.

Zorion grabbed her body in his arms, tearing the last of the wires off her before carrying them both in a flash of pure dragon fire.

Something was wrong. When he landed near the others with her limp body in his arms, he knew all he held was empty flesh. There was no spark of life left in her.

"No!" Naaz yelled, frantic as he knelt by her side. "They had her on life support. She's going to die if we don't help her. Oh, god, we waited too fucking long. Three thousand years to get here. There's no fucking way I'm letting her die now."

"Tell me what will fix her," Zorion said. He pressed his hand to her forehead, the veins lighting with inner fire in his effort to seek out that spark of her soul to tell her to remain. He felt nothing. "She has survived as an immortal all this time. How can she lose that spark now?"

Naaz yanked his sleeve up and took out his knife. With the sharp edge of the blade, he cut a slice across his wrist and held the bloody cut over his sister's mouth. "We had dragon blood in our systems the entire time. Immortal dragon blood. It's how Elites are made. Belah blessed us, and then we were fed either her blood or her brothers' ever since. All it takes is a few drops every few weeks, but we didn't expect this trip to take so long. Neela, please ... drink."

Zorion's darker half landed nearby. The bright orange fire and rumbling concussion of an exploding plane highlighted his change to his human form. He ran to their sides and knelt, taking Neela's limp hand in his.

"Your blood is human," Asha said, grabbing Naaz's wrist. "It won't help her. Your power is dying too. Without my mark and my magic, you wouldn't have survived that fight."

Naaz let out a frustrated yell. "Help her!"

"I have no blood," Zorion said. "And a body without a soul cannot absorb the power I do have. I've tried."

"I have blood but no power to give life," his darker half said. He leveled a piercing stare at Zorion. "We can fix her together, but we have to merge."

Zorion was a hair's breadth from blasting fire at his darker half for suggesting such a thing, but Neela's lifeless body made him restrain himself. He didn't want to damage her. And as much as he hoped to protect her from the memories his darker half held, he would rather she lived with those memories than died.

He stared down at her, brushing his glowing fingertips over her cheek. "Forgive me for this, my love. I will try to take them from you again however I can."

He stood up, and his darker half rose as well, a perfect mirror to his own movements. He'd escaped that dark shell for her sake, but now he had to return to it to save her.

They lifted their hands in unison, palms pressed to palms. Zorion hesitated for only a second when his other half's voice rumbled a warning. "She will be lost to us if we don't do this."

Then all it took was the slightest push of power, and it was as though his entire being had been sucked into a bottomless void. The darkness *did* have power. Enough to steal his will to burn. All the dark memories he'd taken from her haunted him, blamed him for the moment of indulgence he'd taken from her body. He'd had no right, yet she'd agreed willingly out of love for him.

"Snap out of it," the shadow said. "We've got work to do. Help me."

He settled in then, and realized it was more comfortable than it should have been to take over. The shadow remained at the back of his mind, reminding him that they were still at odds.

But when he looked around, the scene before him was wrong. He was greeted by utter silence and stillness; the sounds of the roaring blaze and creaking metal of the destroyed plane had ceased. Both Naaz and Asha stood frozen in place, their worry and grief permanently etched on their faces. His mercenaries were similarly frozen, seemingly in mid-action as they'd been gathering around.

"Did time stop? What is this?" he asked.

"An anomaly. Perhaps just a side-effect in our perception from being rejoined. Don't waste more time we don't have."

He bent and scooped Neela into his arms, and instantly the cacophony of the destruction and the intensity of the scene surged to life once more. Neela's body was still warm, and he could almost believe there was life left in her. There would be again if he had anything to do with it.

"Touch me if you wish to travel with us," he said to the others.

"I don't think you can travel that way inside a body," his shadow warned, but Zorion ignored the voice. Pain shot through his limbs when the power surged at his command to travel, but it subsided just as quickly. Somehow the idea of causing this body pain pleased him, even if he had to feel it himself.

"You were saying?" he murmured when they landed within the chamber he'd shared with Neela the night before.

The shadow remained silent. Zorion laid her on the bed

and the others gathered around. Naaz and Asha had joined them, but the mercenaries who had tagged along politely left the room.

"Give me your knife," he said, reaching out to Naaz.

The worried man handed it over without argument, then pulled Asha close and pressed his face into her hair. She turned in Naaz's arms and kissed him on the cheek, whispering words of comfort. If there was one thing Zorion understood, it was that protective streak a brother possesses. If this didn't work, he had to be prepared for the brother's wrath and accept whatever punishment Naaz offered, though he doubted anything would compare to losing his mate.

He held the knife by the hilt and expelled a bright column of multicolored fire. The flame licked along the blade, coating it with potent magic until the steel glowed white-hot. He stared at it for a second, contemplating the damage he could do to his shadow if he simply plunged the blade into his own chest. She could have his heart's blood from the source. It could save her and get rid of the darkness in the process.

"I love her every bit as much as you do. Take that away from her, and your love is all the weaker for it," his shadow warned. *"Let her choose between us, if it matters so much, but let her live to do it."*

"We split again when this is done and she makes her choice. You'll honor her choice?"

"I will honor her choice."

Zorion pressed the edge of the glowing blade to the fleshy mound of his thumb, carving a circle into the skin. Bright red blood welled up, shimmering with iridescent fire when it began to spill over his palm.

He bent and pressed the cut to Neela's mouth, willing her to taste it, to take in the life-giving power and breathe again for him. For the time together that they had been denied, and that they would take ownership of once she was alive and whole.

Her lips remained still and cold for far too long. No one in the room dared breathe, either. Naaz and Asha clung to each other, watching and waiting.

Zorion bent lower, stroking a hand over her smooth scalp. "You came for me, my Blessed lover. I have come for you. Take me in. Taste my power and live. Please, Neela."

He focused the threads of all his power into the wound, urging more of his fire into the blood that spilled into her mouth. Red fluid seeped out past the corners of her lips, but more made it down her throat. Zorion closed his eyes and focused the power of his fire into that fluid, finding the channels within her body where he could make it flow, first aiming for her heart.

Just as he had with his own incorporeal body, he'd commanded the fire into the remembered human shape he'd once occupied, recreating that shape as closely as possible to mimic what he thought she would expect. He knew the inner workings of his own human shape perfectly, and hers were not much different. His fire pushed through the dormant chambers of her heart, filled it up, and commanded it to beat.

The sound of urgent yelling pulled him back to awareness.

"I'm almost there!" he yelled.

"You're destroying her!" Naaz yanked on his arm and Zorion shook him off, but then his eyes widened in horror as he focused on the bright, molten shape of the woman beneath him. There was nothing but a living, glowing ember where Neela's body had been.

He stumbled back off the bed, the shadow inside his mind howling with grief he could barely comprehend. He smacked into the wall behind him and crumpled to the floor, unable to tear his eyes away as flames erupted from the bedding.

Asha cried out in alarm as Naaz rounded on Zorion, his rage nearly as bright in his aura as the flames around his sister's burning body. Zorion didn't fight, but stood and took every blow. Nothing could hurt worse than his own failure.

CHAPTER 15

NEELA

The sun had never appeared so beautiful as it did today. Neela reached up from where she lay amid the wild, blooming scrub in the field where Zorion had spent the afternoon making love to her over and over. He was asleep beside her, his fiery light dormant.

She wondered if he knew he looked almost human when he slept. His skin turned an opaque gray, his inner fire reduced to a soft glow. He'd left her warm and filled with light from the inside, and she felt an odd kinship with the celestial body that stood watch in the sky above. If she stretched just far enough, she believed she could touch the sun, maybe even capture it and keep it.

"You are a part of me already, child," a warm, maternal voice said. The sun pulsed with a bright orange glow, its heat cascading through her limbs.

"What are you?" Neela asked, not sure she spoke to the sun anymore.

"I am Fire. Your lover called to me to fix you, but your body was too far gone to repair. I have given you a new body. One that honors my true power even more perfectly than the Mother

Dragon's children do. Rise, my child. Burn bright in this new life."

The bright globe of the sun seemed to descend into Neela's arms, its power flooding through her, turning her entire body into light, into pure fire even more powerful than the tightly bound fire Zorion had running through his veins.

Every cell exploded with golden heat, her blood became a molten river, and her breath filled with sparks. When she opened her eyes, the sun beckoned her through the chimney above the burning bed where the ashes of her remains lay. She shot through that opening in a column of fire, and when she reached the open sky, found she had wings that stretched wide, carrying her ever higher.

Neela soared, crying out her elation at this new power and her thanks to the being who had granted her a second chance.

The higher she went, the stronger she felt the tug of something on her soul. At first it was merely a niggling feeling, like she'd forgotten something. As she aimed for the sun itself, that feeling grew and grew, until it pulled taut, yanking her back.

"Why can't I fly to you?"

"The fire that gave you life is not within the sun, my child. It is his fire you must pay homage to. His love resurrected you."

His fire?

Neela arced through the blue sky and looked downward. She stared as though seeing the Earth below for the first time, and far beneath her she saw the glowing ember that was Zorion's fire. Its brightness flickered as though it struggled to remain lit.

He had saved her. He would always save her. But now it was her turn to save him.

She tucked her newfound wings in and aimed down the

way she had come, searching out the chimney she had escaped from and targeting it with the precision of an arrow.

The power of her fire grew as she shot back through the atmosphere, wind howling in her ears as though that other eternal element were cheering on her descent. When she passed back through the skylight, she reined in the brilliant power to avoid blinding the people she loved.

Neela landed amid the dark ashes on the bed, and the pillows ignited instantly. Then the mattress followed, until nothing was left at her feet but a bare, stone slab covered in soot.

"I think we'll need to find another bed, Z."

ZORION COULD BARELY SEE through the swollen flesh of his eyelids, but he kept himself upright, enduring the endless onslaught of Naaz's fists. The other man's face was streaked with tears, but his rage hadn't subsided for nearly half an hour. Beyond him, the fire of Neela's body had burned itself out in a column of light, and Zorion sent a silent prayer along with her soul, wherever it might have wound up. She'd missed the sun so much during her confinement, he hoped perhaps she'd found a place in the heavens along with it.

He'd almost written off the second flash of light as a trick of his failing sight, but when he heard Neela's voice as clear as day, he acted. His hands shot up to block Naaz's fists, catching both of them solidly and holding them immobile.

"Something happened."

Naaz shook his head and blinked. "I'm not fucking done with you yet, asshole."

"Yes, you are. Look."

He forced his eyelids open and focused on the figure that stood amid the flames.

There, standing on the ledge where his bed had been, was the most glorious sight he'd ever seen. The figure was part woman, part fire. Her features were Neela's from head to toe, her skin a rich brown like he remembered, but with an aura of golden fire surrounding her.

No, it wasn't an aura. It was *actual* fire. He went to her, heedless of the heat, leaving Naaz behind to gape at the figure of his sister.

"It worked," he said, though he had no idea how. Inside him, his shadow rejoiced, pushing him to move faster. He reached the ruined bed and opened his arms in time for her to leap into them, her flaming wings stretching out and scorching the stone walls in a pattern that resembled feathers.

He didn't care what happened to his room, his clothes, or anything else. She was alive, and the burn of her kiss was the most exquisite feeling in the world.

CHAPTER 16

NEELA

"*A* fire creature?" Neela asked, her eyes wide and disbelieving. She lifted her hand, and her skin rippled with the inner fire she'd finally managed to subdue enough to avoid igniting everything she touched. "You're saying I died and came back to life … like a phoenix?"

She turned to look at the crowd of people in the room. Her brother's haggard appearance made her want to go to him, but he still bore the bright welts of burns from the first time she'd tried embracing him. Asha's breath was slowly healing him.

Zorion seemed strangely distant, but he answered her question. "Your soul was gone. I failed to protect you, and you were taken. The enemy needed your body alive, but not your soul. I tried to reach you with my fire, but … you were gone. There was truly nothing there."

"Well, I'm here now. And this …" She lifted her arms above her head and craned her neck to ogle the bright, fiery plumage that stretched to either side above her. "This is pretty fucking awesome."

She dropped her gaze to Zorion again, grinning wildly.

She felt alive. More alive than she'd ever felt, even after that first taste of dragon blood that had imbued her with more power than she'd ever imagined.

Zorion looked stricken. "You died to become this, Neela. You should never have been in that much danger. Not while you were with me. If I had only heard you. Heard that you wished for something different … I must remedy my mistake."

She walked toward him, marveling at this new figure who stood before her—Zorion made whole. The physical form he occupied was solid and strong, with deep, ebony skin that shone in the reflected light of her wings. He was more than just fire now. He had flesh and bone and the fire was contained within, though she still saw glimmers of his power pulsing beneath his skin where his veins were closest to the surface.

The best part was that he didn't flinch when she reached out to touch him. Her brother's skin had singed and blistered in an instant, but Zorion was impervious to her fire.

"I forgive you," she said, but frowned when she saw the warring conflict in his eyes. "Don't you want me now? Is this too much for you?"

The heat of her power waned, the glow subsiding as her confidence in his love wavered. He couldn't be harmed by her new power, so why did he hold back?

In her periphery, Naaz and Asha quietly departed, seeming to sense the private nature of this conversation.

"We want you, Neela. But having us might destroy you."

"Dying didn't destroy me," she said in a shaky voice. "What makes you think I can't survive you? And what's this 'we' shit? You got your body back. That's good, right?"

The lights beneath Zorion's skin blazed hot, the same as her skin did without her even trying. His irises flashed and he arched his neck back and let out a yell. Neela's heart pounded as she watched her lover's body begin to oscillate in a blur of pure light. She thought her vision had gone wrong for a moment when she saw two of him standing in front of her, but blinking didn't clear it up.

She shook her head and looked again. There were still two, but one was a solid, dark figure of sculpted black, the other a reflection of him, but crafted of a meshwork of fiery tendrils. That was the Zorion she'd first met, first made love to.

"Who are you?" she asked, addressing the one that lacked the fire.

"I am Zorion's flesh and shadow," he said. "He is the fire and the power."

She turned to look at the other one. "Is this true?"

"Yes. I told you I left all the darkness behind. I rejoined with him to save you, but coexisting within the same shell no longer feels natural. I left the darkness behind for a reason. You don't need to accept it, either."

"Which one of you came to me the first time ... which one of you took the hurt away?"

The darker one looked at the fiery one. "We were whole then. He acted as the shield for your mind, while I absorbed the damage."

"When did this ... split happen?" She waved her hand in the air between them, still trying to comprehend that the man she'd loved for so long wasn't just one man anymore.

"We couldn't protect you from the biggest hurt," the Zorion made of fire said. "The day your captor came and stole the fire of new life from inside you, we fought. We tried to take that pain, but it wasn't only your pain to take. He wanted to protect you. I wanted to protect the child. In the end, we could do neither.

"It wasn't until shortly after when we were moved to the new temple that I separated from him. There were no more temporal wards to keep me bound to him. I couldn't stray beyond the boundary of the tether, but I didn't have to be a part of him anymore. I didn't have to bear witness to the darkness he'd become."

Raw emotion choked her. "That darkness saved me, Z. Both of you saved me. Why can't you be okay with that? He's as much my mate as you are."

"We can't be one dragon for you, Neela," Zorion said. "We are too different now. I can't bear to see you ... subjugated."

"What, and he can?" she snapped. She looked at the dark one. "What does he mean?"

The shadow Z dipped his head. He lifted his shoulders, then let them fall. "Your pleasure is all I wish for, Neela." He raised his gaze and met hers with eyes as black as midnight. "But I want to draw it from you while you are bound and at my mercy."

"You have to choose," the fiery Z said, but Neela's gaze remained fixed on those dark eyes, and he didn't look away either.

"It's my nightmare that made you this way, isn't it?" she asked softly. She stepped close and placed a hand against his cheek. He kept his gaze fixed on her face and nodded. "Show me."

He turned to look at the fiery Z. "He would rather I didn't."

"Fuck what he wants," she spat. "Did you know he held me down the first time?" She shot a blazing stare at the other Z, whose eyes burned right back at her. "You liked it, and so did I. I want to see what makes your dark half tick, because it can't be any worse."

"Neela, don't," he said, moving in and grabbing her hand to pull it away from the shadow.

"Show me, or I am leaving you both."

His heat merged with hers at her back, but he relented,

letting his hands rest on her shoulders as though prepared to pull her away from his reflection at a moment's notice. The shadow Z raised both hands, cupping her cheeks gently.

"It is our darkness, my love," he said, lowering his face to hers.

When their lips met, memories flooded in of all the countless times she'd lain on her back with limbs bound and feet in stirrups. Aside from the first panicked turul, she hadn't seen her partners for those encounters. The blindfold made it impossible to know, but she'd felt every single one.

Except inside these memories, she could see and feel everything. And it wasn't the horror she had braced herself for. In every instance, she gazed up into the face of this dragon who stood before her, his dark eyes taking away her pain, her humiliation, her lack of control, and giving her back what she'd lost. She may have been bound in the memories, but he followed her commands.

"Fuck me," she said in every one, and the figure did as commanded. Her gag fell away and her voice rose loud and clear, every figure that surrounded her falling to their knees while only he remained—his cock at the ready to fulfill her wish.

Neela's body lit up at the vision, and the entire room brightened and the fire inside her blazed with renewed heat.

"Neela, you don't have to accept it," the fiery Z said into her ear from behind. "You can leave that darkness behind."

"No," she said. "It's *my* darkness, and I will fucking own it. I know you liked it as much as I did. If you want to keep me, you will let me have this."

She smiled up at the onyx eyes that gazed down at her. His lips curled into a smile and he looked past her shoulder with one brow raised. She turned in his arms to gaze up into eyes like the sun, her heartbeat fluttering at how much this side of him embodied everything she'd felt during their silent moments sharing thoughts and dreams.

The shadow Z behind her shifted closer, his arms encircling her torso and his mouth brushing her neck.

Z looked hurt and uncertain. Neela raised a hand to his cheek, and their fire seemed to merge, his veins crackling beneath the white heat that flowed from her palm.

"You are a part of me as much as he is, Z. Please don't turn away from me now. I want this. I know it may not feel right to you that I should, but it's my *right* to want this."

"He wants it too, but he denies it," the shadow rumbled into her ear from behind. Her skin sparked beneath his touch as he drifted his hands over her shoulders and down her arms, gripping her by the elbows and forcing her forearms behind her back. The movement caused her bare breasts to push forward against Zorion's chest. She'd tried to put on clothes, but nothing survived coming close to her skin. Nothing but these two men.

Because they were two now—as different in demeanor as night and day. Despite the difference, Zorion had to know there was no choice to be made between them. They were equally hers. She'd waited her entire life to have him, and it didn't matter a bit that the man she'd been bound to from the start was now split into two aspects.

There was darkness in the fire that had made her live once more, just as there was light within the shadow who had shed his blood to revive her. She had no idea if they'd be able to be one again, but she would happily take them as they were, as long as they accepted that they would have to share her.

Zorion's eyes flamed bright, his struggle real amid the power that blazed inside him. She kept her gaze fixed to his, challenging him to give into the desire. A hand slipped up the back of her head, gripped the base of her skull, and pulled back, baring her neck to the figure in front of her.

He tilted his head, his bright gaze flitting over the bared skin of her throat, hunger growing to a fever pitch as his eyes drifted over her. Then he lifted a hand and cupped her face, bending low and hovering with his mouth so close to hers she could feel his hot breath.

"We should take this somewhere more contained," he said. "Don't want to set the entire world on fire."

He tilted his head to the side where Neela caught sight of flames licking across the back of a wooden chair. The table beside it was singed black already just from their proximity.

"Where?" she breathed.

"Anywhere you like."

"Somewhere I can see the sun."

He reached past her and clasped his hands around his shadow's wrists. An instant later, they were in sunlight, though she had no idea where. It had been night in Australia when they left.

She blinked up at a cloudless blue sky, the bright orb of the sun beaming down upon them. They were standing on a solid stone island that appeared to be in the center of a small lake, with a waterfall crashing down into it at the far side. The island was perfectly circular, and beneath her feet was an elaborate carving that depicted a cycle of six dragons, surrounding a glowing circle that pulsed with multicolored light.

"Where are we?"

"Home," Zorion said. "Our fire can't damage this place."

"Good," she said, shivering at the sensation of cool lips brushing over her shoulder from behind. She tilted her head and they both took her invitation, one teasing his mouth across her jaw, the other biting lower down. Her arms were still pinned at her lower back, but she could feel the hot brush of skin against her fingertips and struggled, reaching for more contact with Z's shadow.

"You want to feel my cock?" he asked, and obligingly pushed his hips against her hand. His thick length rubbed along the center of one palm, and she closed her fingers around him. She squeezed until he let out a harsh grunt into her ear, then pulled away again. "That's all you get for now. No more touching until we say so."

"What is this place?" she asked. Though she relished the sun streaming down above, the exposure was new to her.

"Where I was born," Zorion said. "The Dragon Glade. And if you're worried about us being seen, no one's here but us. My parents and aunts and uncles are busy. We'll join them when we're done with you."

She relaxed and let her head fall back on the shadow's shoulder. He released the hold he had on her from behind and slid his arms around her waist.

"Where shall we begin?" the shadow asked. Zorion's jaw pulsed with light, his expression still deadly serious and tight with pent-up need. Despite it being clear his darker half was fully accepting of his deviant desires, Z's fiery side was the one calling the shots, and hadn't fully given into the idea.

"I'm working on it," he said, nodding toward the horizon beyond the outer edge of the pool.

Neela turned in the direction he'd indicated, where a stone staircase led up a rocky slope bordered by lush greenery. At the top, a structure was taking shape, the rocks seeming to form themselves into columns and platforms, then gradually transforming until a pavilion rested atop the hill. More shapes continued moving within as objects appeared, furniture and plants and intricate decor.

The rapid movements of the construction slowed and Zorion nodded. "Close enough," he said. "Let's go."

He took her hand in his, and the three of them instantly

transported to the foot of the staircase. Neela stared in awe as the finishing touches fell into place. As they ascended, the last few stones making up a wide porch settled themselves with rough thumps, and a pair of glass doors opened wide. The house ... because that's what it was, an actual house seemingly constructed out of thin air ... seemed to float. Every wall was a window looking out into the sky, and above them was a skylight that took up the entire center of the roof.

The sun was high above, shining down into the center of the spacious room beneath, where there was nothing but a wide platform. Upon the platform was a contraption she couldn't make sense of, at first. Crafted of smooth, dark stone, it resembled an alien, bird-like creature, with sturdy legs but with a concave back, its wings lying flat. The ends of the wings curled up near where its tail would be.

When they approached it, her entire body heated at the realization of what it was. Not a sculpture of a bird. It was a bizarre chair, crafted no doubt from the abstracted images drawn out of her own memories.

Zorion left her standing with his shadow and moved to the head of the contraption. The stone shifted fluidly when his hands brushed over the surface, until it looked like nothing more than a simple throne carved out of black opal.

"Have a seat," he said.

His shadow held her hand, assisting her up the steps to the top where she turned and sat. She let her hands rest on the contoured arms, enjoying the cool stone's smooth texture beneath her palms.

"What should I call you?" she asked the dark-eyed crea-ture who resembled the man she loved. "I know him as Zorion ... Z ... But you need a name too."

He squatted down in front of her and dark smoke coiled out of his mouth, snaking its way around her wrists to bind them to the arms of the chair. More wound its way down her legs, tickling along her calves to twine around her ankles.

"I am his shadow. But I am your darkness, Neela."

Her breathing quickened with the gentle stroking of his hands up the insides of her legs. A prismatic shift of light passed over her, and she glanced up to see Z behind her with his hands at the sides of the chair.

"Will you always be separate now? Can I never have you together?"

Z leaned down and cupped her breasts. His lips grazed her cheekbone as he brushed his thumbs over her nipples. At the same moment, his shadow's hands pushed her thighs wider and he bent to press his lips at her core, his tongue darting out to tease between her folds.

"Tell me, would you rather have just one of us now? We can more easily fulfill those dark fantasies of yours as separate creatures than if we're bound into one body. I just need you to promise me this is what you want."

Beneath her back, the smooth, polished stone of the chair seemed to morph, its shape flowing and changing. The arms her wrists were bound to spread and shifted, pulling her hands above her head. The back descended, lowering her body flat, and the legs lifted, raising her feet and spreading them wide.

She inhaled sharply at the familiar position she found herself in. Her gaze fixed high above on the bright sun that shone down, then shifted to the figure that stood at her shoulders still. Her head rested at the level of Zorion's hips, and in the daylight, he seemed made of glass, but she knew how warm and pliant his body felt, and how hard and velvet-smooth his cock was.

She licked her lip at the sight of his rigid shaft, the tip shining with a droplet of liquid fire. Then she glanced down her torso to the figure who intrigued her most, though he looked almost mundane compared to the fiery half that had rejected him.

"Will you make me yours now?" she asked. "Mark me and fuck me like you own me?" Simply speaking the words made her own newly discovered fire burn hotter. Something instinctual told her she couldn't truly be tamed now ... you couldn't *own* an element as pure as fire, after all. But without their control, their love, she had a very real fear of burning *too* bright. Bright enough to destroy the things she loved without even trying, just like she'd managed to burn her brother when she'd been resurrected into this new creature.

The shadow half of her lover pushed her legs farther apart, and the chair morphed again to accommodate the change. He moved in between her thighs, brushing ebony knuckles over her mound and dipping one finger between her folds. Her body lit up from that single stroke.

His obsidian eyes flashed with whatever dark fire he still possessed. The piece that Zorion hadn't taken for himself ... the darkness she longed to have a taste of.

"Show us how hot you can get before you beg," the dark half of her lover said. He pressed his thumb to her clit and rubbed, making her cry out at the sudden jolt of pleasure that shot through her body. She was spread wide, completely exposed to him, but the air and sunlight that bathed her skin only made the fire burn hotter.

Zorion's fiery half moved from her head, trailing a hand down her breast and squeezing as he moved to stand at her feet. He crossed his arms as though he intended to observe. His cock still stood proud and hard between his thighs, that burning droplet of fluid still shining at his tip. She longed to taste it, wondering if it would burn her tongue the way it had the first time she'd tasted him, or if her new body could simply absorb all his heat.

She looked back at the shadow, who she'd begun to think

of as *Zil*, "shadow" in her native tongue. His gaze was fixed between her thighs, where he continued slowly rubbing her clit with the pad of his thumb. Heat radiated from that point of contact, as though he'd found a faint ember at her core and sought to stoke it into a raging inferno. Her body brightened with each stroke, her thighs quivering as he brought her closer and closer to the edge of combustion.

"No, Zil, I'll hurt you." She bucked her hips and whined as the pulsing flood of molten heat gathered between her thighs.

"Zil, eh? Is that my name? I take it you acknowledge I am separate from him now?"

She swallowed hard and looked at them both. They were mirror images, but more like photo negatives of each other. Both men seemed to glow with increasing power the more her own heat grew. Both gazed back at her with lust blazing in their eyes, their cravings barely restrained by the constant flexing of their jaws. Zorion's fire-veined fist clenched near his cock as though he ached to touch himself.

"You forget we are dragons, born from the union of two immortals, Neela. Your fire might be divine, but it can't harm us," Zorion said.

"Are you sure? Which one of you is willing to stick your cock in me to find out?"

She wasn't lying about her worry, but the taunt came out anyway. She ached to have one of them inside her—she didn't care which, but she felt like she was about to literally catch fire if she didn't get relief.

Zorion let out a low-pitched growl and grabbed Zil by the shoulder, yanking him back. The shadow chuckled as he stumbled and caught his balance.

Neela didn't care, because her lover wasted no time. He aligned his tip with her entrance and speared her to the core, every inch of his thick length sending hot friction through her body. She arched her back and cried out, rejoicing at the first shove of his cock into her tight sheathe. He leaned over her, grabbing at the contoured edge of the chair above her shoulders for leverage as he fucked her, his eyes white-hot.

"I'm already made of dragon fire, love. The same fire that you're made of."

"Oh god, Z. Please don't stop."

"Never."

His steady, violent thrusts pushed her closer and closer to her peak. As she arched into his probing mouth, another mouth clasped over hers, and Zil plunged his tongue between her lips. He was cool and smooth, just the way she imagined a shadow might taste and feel. She drank him in, realizing for the first time how parched she was and how easily he quenched a thirst she hadn't known she had. With each sweep of his tongue inside her mouth, her heat subsided a bit, but her pleasure continued to grow.

He pulled away and stared down into her eyes, his dark orbs as endless as the night sky.

"Let us taste your fire, Neela," he whispered against her ear, then brushed his cool lips along the side of her throat.

"Let me taste you," she said, the words almost a plea as she twisted her head to try to see his erection.

He glanced at his counterpart. Zorion ceased his steady thrusts just long enough to sear the shadow bindings and flip her over. Beneath her, the chair seemed to anticipate the change, its surface rising up to support her from the front, leaving a smooth, round hump where her hips remained poised. Zorion slammed back into her from behind, hard enough to make her cry out.

Zil caught her chin in one hand and caressed her jaw, sliding a thumb between her teeth. His skin was tangy-sweet, and she realized that was the thumb he'd used to stroke her earlier. He pushed the digit between her lips and she sucked it in, her mouth salivating for even more of him.

Her hands remained free and she realized she could touch him now. She reached for his hips and he grabbed her hands.

"No touching. Mouth only, love."

He pressed her hands tight to the edge of the chair while he positioned his hips before her so that the tip of his cock brushed her lips. The musky tang of him was nothing like his counterpart. Zorion had tasted like fire and light, and his flavor had seemed to melt the second it hit her tongue. Zil was heavy, dark, earthy, and cool.

She opened for him and let him guide her head down over his solid, black length. The veins along his shaft shimmered with subtle violet color as she opened up, swallowing him inch by inch. When he let out a low groan and his hips twitched, she had to restrain herself from smiling.

Zorion's hands were at her hips now, squeezing and yanking her back with each thrust of his cock. Every plunge sent her closer to the brink, but she didn't care about her own climax now. She wanted nothing more than to feel them both spilling their power into her.

But it was a struggle to remain focused with Z's relentless fucking. She let out a helpless whine around Zil's cock as her body began to quiver on the edge of release. Zil stroked her cheek and kept thrusting into her mouth, his tip grazing the back of her throat.

"Just a little more." He brushed a hand down her chest, and the stone support she was propped on seemed to melt away, then grew solid again just beneath her breasts. Zil dropped one hand and tweaked her nipple hard, then switched to the other, repeating the action until fire bloomed through her chest, the tingling heat pushing her to the razor's edge.

The first tickling wave of her orgasm began at the tips of

her breasts and then shot straight to her core. A whining keen erupted from her, barely audible around the still thrusting cock in her mouth.

"Take it, baby," Zil said. "All those nights I saw you bound, I knew if only I could be there, I could make it right. I would have burned them all alive and taken you where you lay. The way he's taking you now. Are you ready to swallow what I have to give you, *adara?*"

Neela had no capacity for coherent thought. She would do anything they desired. Her body reborn of dragon fire belonged to them, and always had.

She nodded as well as she could and Zil let out a harsh grunt, resting his hands on her head. His cock pulsed against her tongue and she gripped the base, holding him still while his semen shot hot and sweet down her throat.

Behind her, Zorion let out a roar, and just as her entire body seemed to burst into flames from the pleasure, his own fire flooded into her.

Zil's shining black torso turned bright red from the fire reflected on his skin. When his climax subsided, Neela pushed back against Zorion, raising up on her knees and writhing her hips to draw the pleasure out. He wrapped hot arms around her and held her close as he continued thrusting, riding out the last little jolts of their orgasms together.

His lips brushed her ear and he sighed a moment later. "He was right," he said, tilting his head to the dark figure who regarded them from the other side of the chair. "I am just as dark as he is on the inside. It is good that you already died, because what I truly wish to do to you might kill you."

The suggestion made an involuntary shiver of anticipation pass through her, and she caught the wicked gleam in Zil's eyes.

"Bring it on, boys," she said.

"Are you willing to test your limits?" Zil asked. He stroked the surface of the chair and it began to morph once more, flattening out on top and rising higher.

Zorion released her without protest as what had become a pedestal of sorts raised her up to shoulder height. She crouched on her knees, hands flat on the surface, looking over the edge at them both. "Are you trying to test my fear of heights? Because I have wings now, remember?" She stretched her fiery plumage out and shook her feathers at them. Sparks floated through the air like glowing confetti.

"Not quite," Zil said. "But this is something I think Zorion and I will agree we should be joined for."

She looked to the other side where Zorion stood frowning. "Is there something that can put you two back together?"

"A common goal, that's all," Zorion said. "I could not mark you before, because I am missing the implement required to do so."

"And I'm unable to make use of said implement without the fire to make it work," Zil said, his voice now coming from a different angle.

Neela spun around again and gasped at the sight of the enormous obsidian scaled dragon that loomed before her. A long, black tongue darted out from between his teeth, tickling suggestively at her bare breasts.

"We must merge to mark you," Zorion said.

Neela was too mesmerized by the majestic creature to answer. She leaned into the teasing flicks of his tongue, tilting her head back and pushing her breasts out to offer them to him. He obligingly licked and teased at each hard tip, then stopped when a throat cleared.

Neela frowned and scowled down at the glaring fire-creature who she loved more than life. "So get on with it, Z. I want you no matter what shape you're in. Dragon shape, man shape, fire shape. All three at once … Can you be all three at once?" She brightened perceptibly without meaning to.

Zil let out a deep, resonant chuckle. "I fear we cannot. Two we can do, but a dragon, a fire man, and a shadow could be arranged." He let out a puff of black smoke that slowly condensed into a man-sized shape. The shape hovered before her in the air, its smoky erection bobbing before her lips. It cupped her cheek, its touch as soft as velvet as he traced a line down her chest to her nipple.

Neela bit her lip and pushed her chest into his touch. Her nipple brightened with heat at the teasing flick of his finger. The fingertip glowed bright orange, then the entire smoky figure suddenly burst into flame, disappearing in an instant.

"Aw, what happened?"

Zil and Zorion both laughed. "You're a little too hot for even smoke to survive, love," Zorion said. "Now turn and let us see those wings so we can decide where to put this mark."

CHAPTER 17

NELEA

*N*eela ignored the order long enough to watch Zorion rest his hand on the dragon's flank and witness the power he embodied flow effortlessly into its hide.

The image before her flickered disconcertingly, as though the dragon's position had changed without her seeing it. His big head had been at eye level to her, then a second later was high above, his neck stretched to its limit. She blinked to clear her vision, worried something was wrong with her head.

"How did you do that?" she asked.

"Did you sense something different?" he asked. "We thought it was just us, but when we merged, it was as though you were frozen for a moment."

"I didn't feel anything, but you definitely did something strange. Can you do it again?"

He lowered his big head again, and the strange oscillation she'd seen before turned his shape into a blur. A moment later, Zorion emerged as the man-shaped network of fiery veins again.

"It seems to occur when we merge," he said. He reached for Zil's scaled flank again, and once more Neela watched as Zorion's body flowed into the dragon's skin.

A sudden searing sensation erupted at the base of her collar bone, and she let out a yelp and placed her hand over the spot. Glancing down, she saw a tiny scrollwork design etched into her skin.

At the sound of low laughter, she looked up, bewildered and disconcerted by the experience. "What the hell happened?"

"It seems that when we merge, time stops," he said. "It's brief, but in that time, we were able to leave a small mark on you. You didn't see us move, did you?'

"No … is this the mark?" She traced her fingertips over the design.

"That is just the beginning, *adara*. Turn and let us see your wings." His eyes flashed with multicolored fire, and his long forked tongue flicked out to lash at her hip.

She obliged, spinning on her knees and fanning her new wings out wide. The stretch felt nice, and she rolled her shoulders, pleased by how perfectly balanced they were, despite their weight.

"Hmm, I can envision the pattern perfectly," Zorion said, and Neela looked over her shoulder at him.

His head was tilted to the side, his long tongue tickling the air as though tasting it. The very tips of both forks of that agile appendage glowed brightly with the power.

She straightened up and smiled coyly, arching her back and spreading her thighs a bit more to ease some of the heat in her core that had built again. His nostrils flared and he shifted his big bulk higher so he practically loomed over her. When he moved, she caught sight of the massive erection that jutted up between his thighs, and the sight made her even hotter.

"What are you waiting for?" she breathed, wishing he would get on with it so he could get back to violating her willing body some more.

He let out a dark puff of smoke that swirled around her, cooling her heated skin and leaving her tingly all over. She glanced down at the iridescent sheen he'd left.

"To numb the pain. It looked like the first mark hurt," he explained before leaning down and brushing his big snout against her nape. He let out another quick gust of breath that enveloped her scalp. Her skin tingled and warmed, and then silken strands tickled the sides of her face. She gasped, reaching up to feel her head.

"You gave me hair again?"

"I enjoy the way it betrays how well fucked you are after I finish with you. And it gives me something to grip when I need to control how you move."

He traced a sharp talon along the line of her shoulder and curled one of the strands around its tip. It wasn't the same deep black she'd had before, but was as variegated with fire as her wings were. He dropped the strand and resumed nuzzling at her neck, his breath sending warm shivers down her spine.

"Your mark will be a dual brand, half mine, half my shadow's," Zorion said. "Beginning at the core, where the power lies, the fire that joins us ..."

Neela bit her lip at the sensation of his tongue tracing a tickling line down her spine. Then in a flash like a whip had struck, that line of pleasure became pain.

She cried out, but the cloud of smoke he blew out soothed the pain in seconds.

"The wings that mirror a dragon's wings are what you share with him," Zorion said, and his tongue sliced more intricate patterns into her shoulders, designs that swirled around the joints of her wings, extending partway up the edges of her feathers.

Again the pain burned bright, but was soothed by his smoke.

"And the darker fire that all three of us crave ..." His tongue smoothed down her back without cutting until he reached her hips. The pain sliced sharp again, and this time she was ready, but somehow the fire was less painful than arousing, perhaps owing to the way he slowed his strokes, his tongue passing more gently from one side to the other in some kind of intricate scrollwork that crisscrossed in the center of her back each time. His strokes moved lower and tightened with each pass, until the very tip of his tongue swiped at the top of her cleft.

She reflexively spread her legs wider, bending to give him more access. Despite the pain his tongue had caused, the cooling layer of magic smoke that still coated her had made an erogenous zone of her entire body, and she wished for those sharp stripes of fire just to feel the magic ease their heat once more.

His tongue didn't stop at the peak of her cleft, but slowed to the lightest tickling touch. Was he still marking her? She couldn't tell, but if he was, she didn't want him to stop.

She leaned forward onto her hands, baring her ass to him. A fresh puff of cool smoke gusted between her cheeks, the sensation like cool tendrils of fog just as soft as that smoky figure's touch had promised to be before he'd been incinerated by her desire.

The twin tips of his tongue glided down between her ass cheeks, skirting the most sensitive parts, but teasing just enough to make her temperature rise and more molten heat pool in her core. She was so hot, she couldn't tell whether his tongue was still doing its magic or he'd simply gotten distracted by her offering.

His tongue slipped lower, still carefully tracing the outer edges of her spread pussy with such precision, she realized he must be adding to the mark. The idea of having it extending all the way around that part of her made an involuntary moan rise up in her chest, and her wings shook. When his tongue reached all the way between her thighs and continued almost to her navel, she was sure of it, because at the end, he backtraced a line of white heat in another intricate pattern right over her womb that he left throbbing with quiet agony.

He pulled his tongue away, and his hot scaled snout brushed at her core. "Your womb is mine now, Neela. No child conceived within will ever be taken again."

Emotion flooded her and tears pricked her eyes. "You know. I thought you were gone that day."

"I was with you, but Meri was stronger than the shade of my mind could overcome."

"She had to mind control me to take the baby. I'd have died to protect my child, if she hadn't."

Another soft gust of smoke surrounded her, and the pulsing heat started to subside.

"No. I want to feel it. Don't take that pain away from me just yet, please."

"Very well," he rumbled. "But I find myself enthralled by this side of you, now that your lovely petals are gilded by fire. Even my shadow can't resist the urge to see you spread wide by our shaft. The cock we share in this form aches for that warm haven."

She looked over her shoulder again, and he was once more gazing down at her with head tilted, his eyes fixed at her core that tingled with heat more intense than simple desire would have produced.

She gave him a playful grin. "Did you mark my pussy, you filthy dragon?"

A dark black cloud puffed from his nostrils and he narrowed his eyes. A deep chuckle rumbled up from his big chest and he rose up and hovered over her.

"I only marked what is mine," he growled against her ear, and she gasped at the feel of the broad tip of his hot javelin of a cock pressing right at the aching opening he'd branded.

Breathless with need, she said, "Then you'd better finish what you started."

She reached up behind her and hooked both hands around his neck, anchoring herself to him and arching her back. At the same moment, his hips tilted closer and his cockhead pressed at her tight channel. She stretched a little, her pussy too tight to take him easily, but the fire burned hotter, searing fluid flowing to coat his head and run down her thighs. A little more of him slipped into her, and she cried out at the intrusion, clinging tighter to his head.

His snout dipped lower over her shoulder, his tongue flicking out and more bright lines of fire covered her chest. It distracted her just enough from the invasion at her core for him to push deeper. Then his tongue traced delicate, fiery flowers around the tips of her breasts, and her entire body lit up. She yelped when he thrust hard, bottoming out in her and letting out a loud roar of triumph when she took all of him.

He began to pump, slowly at first, then with quicker, rhythmic thrusts, each push into her punctuated by another lash of his tongue over some part of her body. He didn't stop at her breasts. Once they were adorned with glowing patterns of dragon fire, he continued down her torso, linking the design beneath her navel to an unfurling motif. She didn't need to see it to feel its beauty as it sank into her skin, marking her with his very essence, and the brand meant all the more to her because it was their shared effort to make her theirs.

Even though it was a single dragon cock that drove deep into her, she was under no illusions that they were of a single mind. For every bright symbol of fire that he etched onto her skin, the shadow countered it with a darker one that balanced the fire and reminded her of her resurrection.

Blood sacrifice, death, rebirth. That was what Zil's marks meant, and as their bodies merged with the ever more violent pounding of his cock, she recalled the other shadow that had lingered inside her that fateful day. His shadow, the silent watcher that had always been beside her. He couldn't take that one memory because he'd known it was one she would never want to forget. Because she needed to be able to remember her daughter when they found her again.

He left no part of her unmarked by the end. Even the contours of her cheeks had tiny threads of fire where he'd ghosted delicate licks along her hairline and at the edges of her jaw. And when his thrusts deepened, her entire body lit up even brighter than before.

"Mine always," he growled against her ear, but within that voice was an echo of a darker voice speaking the exact same words.

"Yes!" she cried, as much in affirmation of their dual claim as her encouragement of the increase in their tempo, until the world went pure white and she found herself soaring high above the building they were in. The sun still hung higher, but nothing but blue sky surrounded them. Her wings stretched out, but something bigger, stronger, held her aloft, and she looked back to see massive black wings stretched wide on either side. But the body the wings were attached to was human-shaped now.

He slowly turned her in his arms until their eyes met. There was love and wonder within, but also conflict. Two men looked back at her from the single pair of eyes, and they seemed uncertain.

"It's all right," she said, stroking the cheek of the face that seemed on the verge of splitting into two. Zorion's fire-veined image was superimposed atop Zil's sculpted obsidian features. "I don't understand why you need to be two, but I'm fine with it. Can you both fly, or do we need to land for you to separate?"

They seemed to exhale a long sigh, and a moment later, only the wicked smile of Zil faced her. At her back was the warm press of another body.

"I don't have wings, but I can be wherever he is, if I wish," Zorion said. "And as long as he is with you, that's where I'll be."

The strange little flowing stone chair had transformed itself into a huge bed by the time they landed. Neela fell into the shimmering softness of it with a sigh. It didn't even occur to her to worry about setting things on fire until she burrowed down and caught a glimpse of her wing out of the corner of one eye, the tiny flames tickling at the pillow. She sat up with a curse, but settled again when she realized nothing showed any sign of being singed.

"This is the Dragon Glade," Zorion said. "No need to worry about combustion up here. Nothing burns unless we wish it to."

"That's a relief, but I am admittedly a little *burned out*. Can your sister find this place? Or are she and Naaz stuck back in that bunker of yours?"

"They are here," Zil said as he settled down on her other side. "She's testing her ability to craft her own abode across the clearing by our mother's house. We will rest. Tomorrow is the Equinox when power in the world will be at its peak."

"Already?" Neela said, her eyelids drooping. "You didn't

have to make it so hard to get to you, you know. We could've had more time together before going back to work."

"I had other plans then," Zorion said. "I apologize for that."

She let out a sigh and rolled over, swinging her leg across his hips and patting him on the chest. "I forgive you. So, what's the plan?"

She groped behind her blindly, hunting for the other half of the pair of mates she'd wound up with so unexpectedly. Zil's cool skin slid beneath her palm, and a second later, he curled his arm around her waist, brushing his lips along her shoulder.

"To test this new power we have. We can apparently stop time when we merge, so we need to learn the limits of it, and find some way to exploit it in our favor ..." Zil trailed off as he seemed to grow fascinated by the weight of her breast in his hand.

"And use it to help destroy our enemy," Zorion finished.

"But before we do, I've got plans to torture her a little," Zil said.

"Oh, I like that plan." Neela smiled and shifted her backside against Zil's hips, interested in the conversation, but entertaining a rising curiosity about how it would feel to have two cocks fucking her at once.

"Yes," Zil said. "Meri has secrets we could all benefit from knowing, especially what she has done with your child."

Neela let out an involuntary sigh, partially in agreement with Zil's sentiment, and partially in pleasure at the way his cock had hardened and was now pressed between her cheeks.

"Are there any secrets you would like to know, *adara?*" Zorion said, touching her chin and urging her gaze to his. His expression was a little playful, though heated, as though he already knew the answer to his question.

She bit her lip, not quite willing to answer.

Zil pushed his cock against her cleft, his tip already slick from his own escaping arousal. She moaned when the head of his cock pushed at her rear opening.

"You hoping to find out what it feels like to experience the dark side, love?" Zil whispered in her ear.

She could do no more than moan her assent.

"How do you feel about light and dark at once?" Zorion asked, shifting onto his side and leaning on one elbow to look down at her.

"I want it all, as long as you two don't mind sharing."

Both of them let out warm rumbles of laughter. "If it's you we have to share, we are more than happy to," Zorion said.

"Good. Now let's see if we can set this place on fire, boys."

Thank you for reading "Dragon Blessed"! If you loved it, please visit the retailer and leave a review!

But wait, there's more!
The Immortal Dragons' quests for mates is coming to an end. Read the epic finale, and Green sister Numa's contest for her mates. Pick up "Dragon Equinox" today, or keep reading for a preview.

And don't forget, subscribing to the Dragon Beasties mailing list gets you **two free sexy dragon shifter stories** not available for sale anywhere.

DRAGON EQUINOX

WITH AN ALL-OUT WAR waging in the Haven over control of the Source, immortal dragon Numa only cares about one thing: securing a powerful enough partner for a taxing ritual that will turn the tides of battle.

But Fate hasn't made her task easy. Rather than show her who her fated mates are to be, the infuriating eternal entity she calls a father has made Numa the prize in a contest of the gods. Whoever wins the favor of Fate's last unmated daughter shall have her as a partner. Numa sees this as an opportunity to secure a lover strong enough to complete the ritual, but isn't prepared when all five contestants unexpectedly capture her heart. Love should not be a factor when her entire world is at risk, so Numa knows she must choose between them.

What does an immortal dragon do when given an impossible choice? She takes them all.

READ ON FOR AN EXCERPT, or buy now.

Chapter One

THE WORLD COULD HAVE ENDED and Bekim Rainsong wouldn't have cared. If there was such a thing as ursa heaven, he'd found it. His entire body buzzed with the immense power that flowed through him, his ears ringing with the sonorous cry of the woman—the dragon—whose glorious orgasm had just shattered his entire concept of what it meant to be *alive*.

"Gaia fucking save me, I can't hold back." Theron's brown eyes were wide with the same wonder, staring at him over the pale shoulder of the woman who was swiftly beginning to mean more to them than their own goddess.

Numa let out a breathy moan between them, her hips still pivoting just enough to drive Bekim mad. "I'm not done yet. If you two hold out a bit longer..." Her green eyes flashed wickedly at Bekim before she kissed him, leaving him even more breathless from the way she owned his mouth just long enough to make him want more. Then she pulled away and twisted, grasping behind her for a very willing Theron, who leaned in and surrendered his own lips to hers as her fingers raked through his short beard.

"How much longer?" Bekim asked, squeezing her hip with one hand while the other cupped the back of her head, urging her back to his mouth.

She laughed into the kiss, her breasts brushing against his chest. "I want to see how much power you two can hold and give back to me. The longer you hold off, the more it builds and builds and, *oh* ..." Her eyes rolled back and her lashes fluttered as her mouth fell open. Inside the tight channel of her pussy Bekim currently shared with his partner, Theron's rhythm had changed, his angle shifting in a way that made Bekim's hold on reality even shakier than it already was.

"Fuck, I can't... Theron, what the fuck?"

His friend grinned down at him as Numa moaned again and pressed her chest flat against Bekim's, burying her face against his neck.

"Going for broke, man. I aim to take her with us when we come. I want another taste of her power, because I fucking swear I felt roots ready to grow under me that time."

"Bullshit," Bekim said, but grabbed both Numa's hips and picked up his tempo to match Theron's.

Numa bit into his shoulder, her fingers sliding up his scalp and pulling at his hair as she let out a sweet little mewl. His partner's cock was a hot, hard piston sliding against his as they rammed into her in tandem.

He and Theron had serviced dozens of ursa females through their estrous since they'd become an official bachelor pair more than a decade ago. Never had the experience been as transformative as this. Numa's skin heated beneath his hands and her entire body seemed to vibrate with a strange subliminal hum that he didn't feel so much as experience from the inside out. It was as though their very souls were vibrating at the same frequency. Theron bent lower over her back, sliding his hands up her sides and clamping them around her shoulders. Bekim recognized the wild abandon in his lover's eyes, the heavy breaths and lowered lids and flushed cheeks above his dark beard that signaled his imminent demise.

"Gaia save me, I fucking love you," Theron blurted just as the hard length of him surged alongside Bekim's cock, signaling his end. Bekim's eyes widened at the outburst, but he didn't have time to dwell on it. Numa's core tightened around their cocks, her teeth released his shoulder, and she arched her back as she cried out her pleasure. The vibrating magic that had danced beneath her skin flooded into him, lighting his entire body up as though he'd been asleep and was only now waking. His orgasm tore through him like wildfire, drawn out with the squeezing pull of her tight sheathe and Theron's cock still pulsing as he released his pent-up climax.

Theron leaned back, looking dazed, his big hands resting lightly on either side of Numa's full, round ass. Numa's face was buried in Bekim's shoulder again and he raised his eyebrows at his partner, mouthing the word "Love?" and pointing his thumb at Numa's back.

Theron gave him a helpless look and a half-shrug. He moved to pull away and Numa's muscles clamped down on them both, eliciting from them a pair of startled gasps.

"Don't go," she said, turning her head to reveal her beautiful flushed face and wet eyes.

Theron patted her gently on the rump. "Not going anywhere but that bed right there beside you, honey. I need to be horizontal for about the next year after that."

Bekim frowned at Numa's green eyes looking up at him. Her eyelids fluttered, her gaze darting away. He hadn't known her long, but in the two months since he and Theron had met her, she'd always seemed every bit the self-possessed immortal, just like all the ursa Shamans. More so, in fact. He'd even go so far as to describe her as *regal*, owing to her color. Gaia's color was green, after all, and he knew that dragon queens were also green. Numa might only be one of the six dragons who ruled the ursa's sister race, but something about her had always elevated her above her five siblings in his eyes.

Not even her red brother had stirred up his need so acutely, and he and Theron both agreed that Gavra had to but say the word and they'd have both happily bowed to his will. Even though their greatest desire was to be chosen by a strong and fertile ursa female, dragons like these weren't likely to cross their paths again.

Numa's sweet kisses, soft curves, and delicious magic put her brother to shame.

She remained flat atop Bekim's chest, his cock still half-hard inside her. Theron flopped down onto the pillows beside them and turned onto his side, sliding his hand down her back, then up in a deliberate caress. It was as though he meant to comfort her, despite the fact that he couldn't have seen the haunted look and the wet lashes Bekim had caught a glimpse of before she pressed her face back against his neck.

He closed his eyes, simply enjoying her warm weight atop him, idly stroking his fingertips up and down her spine with one hand while he sought out Theron with his other. His partner's fingers twined with his amid the bedsheets and squeezed, the touch a signal that they were of one mind when it came to this woman.

"We can't keep meeting like this," Numa said, hoisting herself off Bekim as though her limbs weighed heavy and she'd love nothing more than to stay where she was. Bekim resisted the urge to wrap his arms around her and pull her back down, but his training made him resist. Ursa males took their lead from their females. If she didn't articulate explicit desire for contact, they didn't act, but Gaia help him, she looked like she needed to be held a lot longer than that.

"I have no complaints," Theron said.

"No..." Numa shook her head and slid off of Bekim, retreating to the end of the bed. "It wasn't fair of me to barge into your room like some entitled princess demanding you fuck me."

"We've all had a shitty day," Bekim said. "I think we earned an epic screw after pulling off the impossible."

Numa exhaled a cloud of green smoke that gathered around her as she slipped off the bed and stood, looking down at them. "But we didn't pull it off yet. All we did is confirm *what* we need to do and how to do it. We still have to actually get it done. We still have to find enough power to open a sky portal in the barrier so Nikhil's army can join the war."

"We're ready and willing to do our part. Just say the word," Bekim said. He sat up all the way and scooted to the end of the bed, looking up at her. The green smoke became a solid, sheer wrap that covered her from her breasts to her ankles. The gown was still translucent enough to reveal the lush curves beneath, and the dark pink of her erect nipples showed through. He itched to touch her again, but wouldn't unless she asked.

She gave him a pained look while the smoke tendrils filtered through the messy strands of chestnut hair that fell around her shoulders, untangling and rearranging them into a tidy bun at the back of her head. "It's more complicated than that. You two have been more than accommodating of my needs. But I can't ask you to commit to this with me."

"Why the hell not? We're here, and I don't see that you have a whole hell of a lot of options," Theron said, hopping off the bed and standing beside it with his arms crossed.

"No, but you *do*. Or you will, once this is over and things are back to normal. You two don't need me getting between you and your chance at a normal life with a normal ursa female."

Bekim glanced at Theron, who just gaped at her, speechless. Had she even heard what he'd said?

"I heard your declaration," she said to Theron as if she'd read their minds. "Bekim's a very lucky man. I'd only get in the way of that. I'm already getting in the way of that. Please don't feel obligated to join this ritual with me."

"We're not the ones, are we?" Bekim asked.

Numa stared at him for a beat, her expression guarded as though she was trying to decide how much to say.

Theron picked up the thread of Bekim's question. "Gavra said you all had dreams of your mates. That's why he never shared our bed … he only tagged along on our assignations to take advantage of the excess fertile magic. I take it you didn't dream of us, and you don't want to commit us to the ritual if we're not supposed to be yours. How close am I to the truth?"

Her haunted look returned, and she shook her head and turned away. "Close enough," she said, striding to the door.

"Let us help anyway," Bekim called after her. "We can help you find him, or them, or whoever it is, if you give us a clue."

Her shoulders stiffened when she reached the door, and she stood with clenched fists for a second before turning, a stricken look on her face.

"That's the problem. I don't *have* a damn clue myself. I wasn't blessed with dreams the way my brothers and sisters were. It could be anyone. Or no one."

"But it has to be someone … doesn't it?" Theron asked. "Fate's got to have some idea. You wouldn't be fucking stuck in this situation without some way out."

"I wouldn't be surprised if Fate just doesn't care. I'm the unremarkable daughter … the one who follows the rules, who keeps a level head. I've never sought out attention—never wanted it, really. I did my duty as a goddess from afar for the humans who worshiped me before we were forced to protect ourselves with barriers, portals, and hibernation temples. Maybe I did something wrong and Fate just … forgot."

"Maybe that means you get to choose," Bekim offered.

Numa gave him a sad look. "If that's true … if the decision really is mine to make, then I have to consider what's required of the ritual. Love has nothing to do with it. I need a mate with enough power to open a sky portal in the Sanctuary's barrier. I've spent several wonderful afternoons with the two of you. You have more than enough to keep any dragon satisfied for ages. But nothing short of divine power will be enough for me, I'm afraid ... or at least something close." She speared them both with looks that drove straight to Bekim's heart. "I love you too, but that just isn't enough."

The door shut soundly behind her and Bekim let his head drop forward. He inhaled sharply, gritting his teeth against the agonized yell threatening to burst from him. Theron closed the distance and squeezed his shoulder.

"Her hands are tied. If we want her to open that portal, we have to trust her to know how it needs to be done."

Bekim just shook his head and stared blindly at his lover's feet. After a moment, he narrowed his eyes, finally focusing and for the first time seeing something that made no logical sense.

"Theron ... since when did you start sprouting leaves from your ankles?" He bent down, worried he might be hallucinating, perhaps still high on green dragon magic. His fingertip came into contact with the edge of a pale green leaf that gave slightly under his touch, the little limb it sprouted from solidly attached to Theron's left ankle.

The foot in front of him tilted and turned.

"Holy shit." Theron dropped to the floor, propping his foot up on his knee. He stared at the little sprout that gradually faded and sank back into his foot.

Bekim gave him a sad look. "I guess this means you might have a chance with her after all. If you have Gaia's blessing, you might have enough power to satisfy her requirements for the ritual."

"Dude, you'd better lose that fucking grim expression. *We* have a chance with her now. I might have had a dinky little leaf, but you've got a little more going on than that."

He gestured to the floor at Bekim's feet. Bekim looked down, and it took a moment before the image before him finally registered. It was as though the veins beneath his skin were filled with sunlight, and each one flowed up as far as his ankles, feeding a ring of blossoms that opened up before his eyes. The centers of the blossoms all glowed a vivid green and the aroma of jasmine filled the air.

"Gaia's gift," Bekim whispered. "But we know there's a price … there always is. You remember what happened to Silas."

"And Vrishti helped him find a way around that. But Sathmika unlocked that gift for him. How the hell did *we* get it?"

The early morning light warmed and grew dense with humidity. Both men tensed at the abrupt change and met each other's eyes. Brilliant green light flashed beside them and they both stood, but Bekim found himself immobilized. When he glanced down at his feet, he saw they were rooted to the floor—quite literally—with dark, woody tendrils twisting into the planks.

The light in front of them coalesced into a blindingly beautiful female shape. She was naked, but seemed to be clothed in the long, curling tendrils of her own hair that flowed around her curvaceous body like thick vines. Flowers sprouted from the locks, beginning with a crown of them encircling her head.

Bekim's eyes bulged and he nearly choked on his surprise.

"G-Gaia?" Theron stuttered.

The woman gave him a warm, maternal smile. "Yes, my child. You are correct that there is a price for my gift, but I imagine this is one you would not hesitate to pay."

"What is it?" Bekim asked, finally finding his voice.

"There is to be a contest. A sort of wager between the gods. I have chosen the pair of you as my proxies. Win this wager for me, and you can keep your gift."

He narrowed his eyes. Neither he nor Theron had ever been gambling men, but perhaps that was why they had yet to find a female willing to mate them. "What are the stakes of this wager?"

"The stakes are the same as the prize. Win the dragon Numa's love. Secure yourselves as her mates, and my gift is yours to keep as well."

With that, she disappeared in a cloud of green-gold mist, leaving behind the scent of fresh summer blooms.

Bekim swallowed. "Well, all right then. I don't suppose we have a choice in this, do we?"

"Why would we *ever* say no to this?" Theron asked. "We have a chance now. A really fucking stellar chance, considering we already know how she feels about us and there aren't exactly any other blokes beating down her door. Tell me you feel the same way I do."

"Yeah… you know I do. I love her too, but I can't help but feel like there's a catch."

"Mates, man. We'll be her mates if we do this. Does anything else even fucking matter?"

Theron had a point, and if this was a chance for them to drive away Numa's sad looks, whatever catch would no doubt be worth it.

WANT TO READ THE REST? Buy now.

Ophelia Bell loves a good bad-boy and especially strong women in her stories. Women who aren't apologetic about enjoying sex and bad boys who don't mind being with a woman who's in charge, at least on the surface, because pretty much anything goes in the bedroom.

Ophelia grew up on a rural farm in North Carolina and now lives in Los Angeles with her own tattooed bad-boy husband and six attention-whoring cats.

Subscribe to Ophelia's newsletter to get updates directly in your inbox. If newsletters aren't your thing, you can find her on social media.

http://opheliabell.com/subscribe

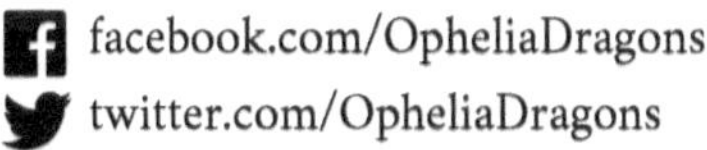
facebook.com/OpheliaDragons
twitter.com/OpheliaDragons

Sleeping Dragons Series

Animus

Tabula Rasa

Gemini

Shadows

Nexus

Ascend

Sleeping Dragons Omnibus

Rising Dragons Series

Night Fire

Breath of Destiny

Breath of Memory

Breath of Innocence

Breath of Desire

Breath of Love

Breath of Flame and Shadow

Breath of Fate

Sisters of Flame

Rising Dragons Omnibus

Dragon's Melody (a standalone dragon novel)

Immortal Dragons Series

Dragon Betrayed

Dragon Blues

Dragon Void

Dragon Splendor

Dragon Rebel

Dragon Guardian

Dragon Blessed

Dragon Equinox

Dragon Avenged

Immortal Dragons Box Sets:

Immortal Dragons: Books 1, 2, & 3 + Prequel

Immortal Dragons: Books 4-6 + Epilogue

Black Mountain Bears

Clawed

Bitten

Nailed

Stonetree Trilogy

Fate's Fools Series

Fate's Fools

Fool's Folly

Fool's Paradise

Fool's Errand

Nobody's Fool

Eye of the Hurricane

Fool's Bargain

April's Fools

Thieves of Fate

Aurora Champions Series

(Set in Milly Taiden's "Paranormal Dating Agency" world)

The Way to a Bear's Heart

Hot Wings

Triple Talons

Midnight Star

Once in a Dragon Moon

Second Skin Series (Romantic Suspense)

Mad Dog

Mile High

Valentine's Day

The Devil's Daughter

Marked Man

Rebel Lust Taboo

Casey's Secrets

Blackmailing Benjamin

Burying His Desires

Doubling Down

~

Standalone Erotic Tales

After You

Out of the Cold

www.ingramcontent.com/pod-product-compliance
Lightning Source LLC
Chambersburg PA
CBHW030637190726
48286CB00008B/2556